Hardening his hold on Sally, Max contained the shiver his kiss had forced out of her

'You have my ring. I've offered you my name. On a purely temporary basis, of course, a condition you accepted. An engagement lasting a few months, maybe even a year, which, as relationships go in these *emotionally enlightened* days—" the emphasis was cuttingly sarcastic "—is as reasonable a length of time as anyone might expect. So let yourself go, suspend your disbelief, as I have. I'm deeply into this role of husband-to-be to you, and in the best theatrical tradition I'm letting the part I'm playing of your lover take over my own character and lead me to its ultimate goal—your bed."

It was like a hurricane, this feeling he was creating inside her, lifting her off her feet and rendering her unable to help herself.

"You've bewitched me, witch," Max said huskily.

LILIAN PEAKE lives near the sea in England. Her first job was working for a mystery writer, employment that she says gave her an excellent insight into how an author functions. She went on to become a journalist and reported on the fashion world for a trade magazine. Later she took on an advice column, the writing of which contributed to her understanding of people's lives. Now she draws on her experiences and perception, not to mention a fertile imagination, to craft her many fine romances. She and her husband, a college principal, have three children.

Books by Lilian Peake

HARLEQUIN PRESENTS

HARLEQUIN ROMANCE

LILIAN PEAKE

Undercover Affair

Harlequin Books

TORONTO • NEW YORK • LONDON
AMSTERDAM • PARIS • SYDNEY • HAMBURG
STOCKHOLM • ATHENS • TOKYO • MILAN
MADRID • WARSAW • BUDAPEST • AUCKLAND

Harlequin Presents first edition February 1993
ISBN 0-373-11532-6

Original hardcover edition published in 1991
by Mills & Boon Limited

UNDERCOVER AFFAIR

CHAPTER ONE

'IF ONLY you'd have enough faith in me to give me the job,' Sally urged, agitatedly using both hands to push back her rich brown hair, 'I'm sure I could prove myself capable of providing you with the story you want.'

Derek Winterton, dark hair grey-shaded, leaned back in his swivel seat, tapping the palm of his hand with a pencil. 'You think that because your uncle's chairman of the board, I should accept you on the editorial staff purely on the basis of his obviously prejudiced recommendation of your capabilities? Plus your own verbal assessment of your ability to do the job?'

Sally nodded.

'OK, so where's your *curriculum vitae*? I want something in writing to back up your argument that you're good enough to take on this assignment for the *Star and Journal*.'

Sally's tongue dampened her lips. 'I——' she cleared her throat '—the only CV I've got is one that's relevant to the career I've just abandoned. As a teacher of English, entering the profession straight from college, I wouldn't have anything on it that's relevant to journalism, would I?'

Derek Winterton rested his elbows on the desk. 'You've had just one employer?'

'One school, yes.'

'Oh-h dear!' The editor sighed. 'Maximilian Mackenzie's a tough nut to crack. Middle thirties, tall, broad and handsome as they come. Dislikes journalists, even though he used to be one himself before he turned

5

to writing political thrillers. Refuses to give interviews. Hardly anything known about his private life, except that the lady he was about to marry walked out on him. According to our files, that was a bit over three years ago.'

'I'm a tough nut too, Mr Winterton.'

'You?' Derek smiled. 'You're how old—twenty-five or -six? With your bush of brown hair, bright matching eyes, not to mention a mouth so sweet it couldn't ever have uttered a single curse...a tough nut?'

'I can get angry, like when the kids at school are difficult, and it seems to bring them to their senses. Sorry, *were* difficult. I left my job three weeks ago.'

'So you want me to say education's loss is my gain?'

'Just try me, Mr Winterton,' she pleaded, 'that's all I'm asking.'

'If I don't, I suppose I'll have your uncle to answer to. And my job to look out for.' He regarded her closely. 'This man's a belligerent subject. He's elusive, to put it mildly. You'd be a green, completely inexperienced pseudo-journalist. And female, at that.'

'Might not that be an advantage? Put the subject of this discussion off guard?'

'Maybe,' reluctantly, 'you've got something. On the other hand, I can't print schoolmarm essays in my paper, which, because of your training, is probably all you can turn out.' She made to protest, but he raised his hand. 'Can't be done, Sally, niece or not of the chairman of the board. Sorry.'

He lifted the phone, mouthed, 'Sorry, Sally,' again and spoke to the person at the other end.

'What I can't understand,' remarked Gerald, his long, thin length reclining awkwardly in Sally's fireside chair, 'is why you're going off on this hare-brained trip. It might have made sense if the editor of the *Star and*

Journal had given you a job, but to go off into the blue just for the hell of it——'

'Fun of it,' Sally corrected. Determinedly she packed two extra T-shirts into her already over-full backpack. 'Don't you understand? I'm twenty-five, coming up twenty-six. There comes a time in everybody's life...' She glanced at her companion's recumbent form. His puzzled eyes were struggling to comprehend, and she added with a sigh, 'No, you don't understand, do you?'

For the two years in which she had known Gerald Farnley, first as a colleague, then as a friend, he had never understood. She knelt on the floor, breathing hard after her tussle with the backpack.

'Why,' Gerald persisted, 'do you have to disappear to the antipodes for heaven knows how long? Why couldn't you have agreed to marry me instead?'

'Gerald,' she put her hand on his knee and he immediately covered it with his own, 'I'm fond of you, but—well, I just wish you could understand——'

But he still wouldn't, she told herself sadly. Nor could she tell him that, affectionate and good-natured though he was, he simply did not touch her emotionally, nor in any other way.

'You need more time, is that it?'

'The world,' she tried to explain, 'in particular the other side of the world, is calling. So I'm using my savings——'

'But you told me that, because of the high rent of the place you were renting, you'd only been able to save enough to buy your ticket, with very little left over to pay for your accommodation beyond the first few days,' Gerald put in worriedly, 'not to mention——'

Sally smiled with more confidence than she felt. 'I'll manage, don't worry.'

Gerald took her outstretched hand. When he had gone, leaving a warm, if moist kiss on her lips, the feeling of freedom swept over her. She stretched luxuriously. Despite her failure to secure a job on the *Star and Journal*, she could not see a single cloud in her particular sky.

If, as she had booked her flight, her reason—and her disciplined teacher's mind—had tried to tell her that taking on a trip as far away and as lengthy as she anticipated, without sufficient funds to see her through, was foolhardy in the extreme, then for once she had firmly refused to listen.

She allowed her thoughts to dwell for a few minutes on the past—her father's long illness, her mother's devotion to him, her own contribution to his welfare in the form of giving all she had both domestically and financially.

There had rarely been anything left over for her to buy necessities, let alone luxuries, but it was not something she ever regretted. Making her father's life as comfortable as possible, and her mother's as trouble-free, had been her sole aim. And, she sighed, staring out at the grey roofs around her, it seemed she had finally succeeded. After years of unhappiness and near-despair at the loss of her beloved husband, her mother was happily married again.

Now it's my turn, she thought. World out there, here I come!

The airport was packed with people all as eager as she was, Sally observed, to get off the ground and on their many and varied ways.

Carrying a loaded tray, in addition to a bulky airline bag, proved to be a physical impossibility. Carefully lowering the bag, she pushed it out of the way of other people's feet. It should, she decided, be safe enough there. When she had found a seat, she would return for it. Shouldering the much smaller backpack which, in the course of her travels, she intended to use as a personal bag, she looked around the crowded cafeteria.

Every nearby table was full, so she made her slow way over stretched-out legs, past airline trolleys and between racing, excited children, to the far side, her eyes roaming around. At a corner table half a dozen steps away a man sat alone. Another chair was pushed in across from him.

Heaven be praised, Sally thought, and made for it, her eyes fixed on it lest it should be grabbed by someone else. She was within touching distance when a tiny child darted beneath her tray. Attempting to shield the child from the scalding contents of the teapot which was poised near the edge, Sally jerked to one side, her foot curling round a table leg. She felt herself falling and thrust the tray high to protect the child.

The sandwich packet tumbled off, while the filled teapot missed by a finger's width the immaculately trousered legs of the man already seated. Sally's knees came down hard against the tiled floor and she gave an involuntary cry of pain. The orange juice shot across the elevated tray and proceeded to pour its contents over the man's equally immaculate shirt and pale grey casual jacket. Only the tray remained firmly in Sally's rigid, horrified grasp. Of the child there was, thankfully, no sign.

'Oh, no!' Sally exclaimed, her lips trembling. Rising awkwardly, she rubbed at her knee, ridding herself of the tray at the same time. The other knee had been cushioned from the bruising fall by landing on the packet of sandwiches. Then she saw the damage the accident had inflicted on the entirely innocent party already seated at the table.

'Oh, heavens, no!' she groaned.

The stains on the man's clothes were busy enlarging themselves, the expensive fabric thirstily lapping up the highly coloured liquid.

'Did you hurt yourself?' the man enquired, to Sally's surprise sparing time from frowningly contemplating the ruination of his clothes to ask after the offender's wellbeing.

'Yes. No. I mean...' She raked feverishly in her blouson jacket pocket and pulled out a handful of tissues.

'Here, please use these,' she offered.

The victim was already attempting to dab himself with his handkerchief. Sally, obeying her instinct to assist, crouched down, her expertise acquired through years of mopping up children after classroom accidents. She pushed his hand away and pressed her paper bundle against him, the better to absorb the liquid before it penetrated too deeply into the light grey fabric.

Before he could protest, she repeated the exercise, moving the tissues across the fine material of his shirt, feeling beneath the pressure she was applying the sinewy leanness of his physique.

'My God, not again!' she thought she heard him mutter.

He jerked away from her ministrations and she looked up at him questioningly. She shook back her hair the better to see him. Their eyes clashed, his flashing with a kind of muted anger. A curious spark of response leapt inside her, but she did not stop, so anxious was she to make amends for the damage she had caused to his clothing.

'I'm sorry, so sorry,' she murmured, as if soothing words could put the damage right, but the man's mouth was compressed, his eyes expressionless as his hand came out and grasped her wrist, levering it away from all contact with his person.

If he objected that much to her touch, she decided, she had better stop trying to achieve the impossible. The stain wouldn't even begin to shift with the ineffective method she was using, so she ceased at once, and rose, face flushed.

Seeing him more clearly now, she felt a jolt of recognition. Hadn't she seen that face somewhere before? Those eyes, cool and blue, that wide forehead topped by a cap of thick black hair, that long, straight nose poised with a faintly arrogant air over a firm mouth—hadn't they all stared up at her from—from some newspaper? Magazine supplement? That was it, that was where she had seen him, but in what context? This was no time, she admonished herself, to delve into her subconscious mind, seeking elusive answers.

'I really am sorry,' she apologised again, but he brushed her conciliatory words aside.

'It's one of those things,' he dismissed brusquely, plainly still annoyed. 'The dry-cleaning bill won't exactly leave me poverty-stricken.'

'Oh, please send that to me,' she begged. 'It was my fault that it happened.'

'No, it wasn't, love,' the lady catering assistant declared, deftly wielding her cloth and her mop, having materialised like a good fairy out of the mêlée. 'It was an accident—I saw it all with my own eyes. It was that kiddy. Little ones get so excited in these places. They race about like baby tornadoes and——'

As she talked, she took Sally's tray, retrieved the teapot from under the table, mopped the spilt liquid and scraped up the remains of the sandwiches on which Sally had inadvertently knelt.

'That's the end of them,' the lady declared with a rueful smile. 'I'll get you another packet, shall I, dear?'

'That's very nice of you,' Sally said quickly, 'but I couldn't afford another——'

'On the house, love,' the assistant said, bustling away. 'You just sit yourself down there,' she indicated the chair opposite the man, 'and I won't be two ticks.'

Gratefully watching her go, Sally turned back to her companion, who was now busy with his once-white handkerchief dabbing at his orange-hued newspaper. 'I really am——' she began, when he cut in,

'OK, joke's over. It was a novel approach, new to me, but no doubt it's worked in the past on others.' He scribbled on a scrap of paper. 'The address of the woman who runs my fan club. She'll give you the blurb you're after, a photograph, anything else you might want——' Her puzzled frown stopped him.

'*Fan club?* What fan club? Would you please tell me what you're talking about? I tripped because I was avoiding that child. Oh, heavens!' Sally gasped, fingers to her mouth. 'My hand luggage, my airline bag! I left it back there, tucked away out of sight.'

'For Pete's sake,' the man growled, 'you left it *where*?'

She rose agitatedly, pointing. 'At the side of the counter. I couldn't carry it plus the tray, so I——'

'Stay right where you are,' the man said grimly, getting to his feet and pushing his way across the cafeteria.

Waiting anxiously, Sally pulled towards her the smaller rucksack, in which she carried her personal belongings. She was certain she had put into it her passport and air tickets, but before she could search the bag thoroughly the man reappeared, stepping over legs, baggage and children as she had done. He was empty-handed.

'Which counter?' he demanded. 'The main one or the smaller one for drinks only?'

'The main one,' she answered, her dismay growing. 'Was that where you looked?'

'I looked around both. No sign of a bag. Are you certain——?'

'Certain.' She mauled her lip, trying to keep down the rising panic. It couldn't have happened to her, it just couldn't!

'Here you are, love.' The lady assistant reappeared, passing across a replacement glass of orange juice and a packet of sandwiches. 'And a nice cup of tea, with my compliments.'

'That's so kind of you——'

'What was that you were saying, dear, about leaving a package?'

Sally explained.

'Don't worry, dear. I expect it was Security. Someone must have reported seeing a suspect bag and it's been taken into custody. All you've got to do is go and see them, and you'll get it back. First, though, eat up, there's a dear, before that lot gets spilt too.'

Sally, weakly smiling her thanks, did as she was told.

'I'll go with you,' the man informed her briskly, as he turned his newspaper inside out, the better to read the unsullied interior pages. 'When you've eaten your——' he lowered the paper and glanced at the meagre spread '—er—meal.'

Between mouthfuls—she was hungrier than she had realised—she thanked him, but said it wasn't really necessary. This he brushed aside and continued with his reading.

'I'm—I've finished,' she said uncertainly, unhappy at troubling the man whose clothes she had almost ruined, yet oddly glad to have his support, 'but, as I said, you needn't bother.'

'No bother,' he said briskly, refolding the newspaper and leaving it on his seat. 'But you will let my fan club know, won't you,' he added sarcastically, 'about my good deed in looking after the interests of one of my devoted fans.'

Sally rose to her full height, tall enough to intimidate misbehaving teenagers, but failing, it seemed, to impress one atom the six-foot-plus length of the object of that fan club he was so certain she belonged to. 'Please believe me when I say that I've never heard of you, whoever you may be, which means that I can't be a fan of yours, can I?'

A faint smile passed across his face at her own heated rejoinder. Picking up her bag, Sally followed the man's decisive strides through the milling throng.

'Name, sir?' asked the man at the Lost Property desk. Sally's companion's tilting head indicated her.

'Sarah Dearlove,' she answered. 'Yes, I did say Dearlove. Spelt exactly as you would imagine,' she added with a patience which told the world in general, and her two listeners in particular, that the spelling of her unusual name had been queried many times.

'A holdall? Also known as an airline bag? Let me look.' The shake of the official's head as he reappeared caused Sally's heart to do a crash dive. 'Nothing's been handed in, sir—er—madam.'

'Oh, heavens,' Sally groaned, 'what shall I do if it doesn't turn up before I leave? There's so much in it that I'll need.'

The official tried to be helpful. 'I'll take your name and address, miss, and contact you if——'

'It's no good doing that,' Sally explained, trying to steady her voice. 'I'll be travelling around for some weeks.'

Her companion glanced over his shoulder at her. 'You could give your home address, in case it's found some time in the future.'

'Home address?' she echoed faintly. 'I—I haven't got one at present. I was renting a place, but gave it up when I left.'

The man frowned, seeming to be turning something over in his mind. 'I'll give you mine,' he said to the official.

Listening intently over the general chatter and loud-speaker announcements, Sally heard the man say, 'My name is Maximilian Mackenzie,' proceeding to give an address in Surrey, the details of which Sally couldn't catch. 'I can always write to Miss Dearlove Poste Restante at a prearranged post office back home. Agreed, Miss Dearlove?'

Miss Dearlove could not but agree. She also went cold all over, then felt the heat of excitement chasing the chill away. This was Maximilian Mackenzie, the man whose story she had so wanted to tackle—as a reporter on the *Star and Journal*, but which position was refused her by the untrusting editor. Now, Maximilian Mackenzie had as good as fallen, like a ripe peach, into her hand!

Why hadn't she recognised him on sight? If her ambition to join the reporting staff of that paper was ever to be realised, her bloodhound instincts would have to be sharpened to a much finer point than this.

Her hazy remembrance of having seen him somewhere should by now have hardened into a positive identification. Hadn't she already observed the man's supreme self-confidence, not to mention his commanding nature? All these, in addition to her faint jolt of recognition on first seeing him, should have combined to give her the answer to his identity.

There was something she had to do without fail, and that was to let the editor of the *Star and Journal* know of her good fortune. He would just *have* to give her that break now. If only she could escape for a few minutes—that was all it would take—and put a call through to him.

'Mr Mackenzie?' The voice was feminine, young and eager. 'Oh, thank heavens, Mr Mackenzie, I've caught up with you!'

A small-built, brown-haired young woman was elbowing her way through the semi-circle of anxious people, all of whom were hoping to reclaim their lost property. 'Mr Mackenzie, are you flying out of the country? Tell me where, Mr Mackenzie, I can't bear to think of you not breathing the same air as I do. Mr Mackenzie, I have a book of yours here. I'd really appreciate it if you'd autograph it for me...'

'Oh, good grief, no!' Sally was astonished to hear him murmur under his breath. Hadn't he said something like that back there, when her glass of orange juice had molested him? She was even more astonished when he seized her shoulder, pulling her to him and placing a warm and unbelievably exciting kiss on her gasping mouth.

He lifted his head, holding her eyes, and their expression seemed to reflect back her own surprise. 'Miss Dearlove, I——'

'Dear love? You called her your dear love?' the young woman exclaimed, seeming ready to burst into tears. 'D-does that mean she's the w-wife you've always denied having? I'll—I'll *sue* that Jennie Smith who runs your fan club for hiding the truth from us! Or,' a little more brightly, 'is she your fiancée, perhaps? Which means you're still legally free?'

Maximilian Mackenzie's glance sliced downward to Sally again. It asked, Are you willing to play ball? Well, she owed him a dry-cleaned suit, not to mention a washed shirt.

By now a small crowd had gathered, a large proportion of which was interested only in pushing its way nearer to the lost property counter, and therefore irritated with the dramatic scene that was being enacted before its eyes.

Yes, Sally's long lashes signalled, I'll play Juliet to your Romeo. She owed him that, at least.

'He's—he's my dear love too,' she murmured to the young woman, who clutched a thick, hardback book to her chest. 'Aren't you, Maximil——?'

'Max to you,' the whisper intended for Sally's ears only prompted.

Gazing fondly up at him, she wound her arm into his. The smile he turned on her melted her bones, although her reason told her firmly that he was play-acting too.

The young woman thrust the book she was holding towards him, offering him a pen as she did so.

'Please, Mr Mackenzie,' she pleaded. 'I've come all this way to try and catch you. The M M fan club secretary told me you'd be here, so I——'

He took the book and the pen, but Sally was certain she heard him growl, 'Damn the fan club!' He raised cool, if not completely unfriendly eyebrows at the young woman. 'What's your name?'

'Henrietta Curzon, Henni for short.'

'Shall I?' asked Sally, offering her hands as support for the book as he autographed it.

'Thanks, Miss—er——' a quick glance revealed the faintest flick of amusement '—dear love.' He had deliberately separated the two syllables of her name.

'Strange,' Henni Curzon said, frowning at Sally's well-worn clothes, then watching Max sign his name. 'Your choice, I mean. Of a wife. She's so—so——'

'Ordinary?' Sally put in with an impish smile, flashing her brilliant brown gaze at the man at her side and pouting her curving red lips as if inviting his kiss. She was glad, then, of the experience producing school plays had given her in the effective use of facial expressions.

'That's right.' The girl accepted the book back with loving care. 'I'd have thought you, Mr Mackenzie, would have gone for the model-girl type—you know, slinky and sexy and full of you-know-what. Still,' she smiled, then sighed, 'it gives the rest of us ordinary girls some hope, I guess, doesn't it?'

'Oh,' said Sally a little wickedly, 'I can be sexy and full of you-know-what when I like. Can't I, Mr M—er—Max?'

In answer he put his arm around her waist and pulled her to him.

'Thanks, anyway,' said Henni. 'I'll treasure this,' holding the book to her, 'even though you've got a wife-to-be now. Anyway,' eyes brightening again with a hope that for her plainly sprang eternal, 'you're not married to her yet, are you?'

CHAPTER TWO

HENNI had disappeared from sight before Max Mackenzie freed Sally from his hold. It was, she told herself, the end, the termination of the shortest and most exciting acquaintance she had ever experienced.

'Thank you, Mr Mackenzie,' she said, shouldering her bag and looking round quite pointlessly, if longingly, for her missing piece of hand luggage.

'Come back to our table.' He gazed across the busy restaurant. 'Miraculously, it's still free.'

'But I really should be——' She glanced at her watch, desperately wanting to find a telephone. Her eyes sought the nearest television monitor displaying flight information. If she didn't hurry...

Max Mackenzie intercepted her glance. 'They announce boarding details over the speakers, Miss Dearlove,' he remarked drily. 'Are you sure you're safe to be let loose in an airport of this size? Any airport, in fact? Which planet have you sprung from to have reached your mid-twenties—am I right?'

Sally nodded.

'—without any flying experience?'

'Wrong,' Sally pointed out with a smile. 'I flew to Holland once. With my parents.' Her eyes clouded. How happy the three of them had been in those days, before her father's illness. 'To see the tulips in bloom. I remember the stunning colours, the beauty of it all,' she added wistfully.

'You were a child? Flying,' he went on with a wry smile, 'has changed somewhat since then. Compared

19

with that journey,' he added reflectively, guiding her back to their table, now cleared of used crockery, 'anywhere in the world is a long way for someone as inexperienced as you appear to be to leave the nest and fly into the unknown.'

'The nest left me, Mr Mackenzie,' she answered flatly, seating herself with some reluctance.

Her tone seemed to have surprised him, her words intrigued him. It was as if he were discovering that, despite her wide-eyed reaction to her immediate and somewhat bewildering surroundings, she was adult after all.

Surreptitiously, she eyed the signs, seeking for the word 'telephones'. There had to be a way... She had it! The most obvious way in the world...

'I hope you'll excuse me, Mr Mackenzie, if I...'

He understood! 'Go ahead. If there's an announcement from Lost Property I'll hear it.'

Hoping she had mixed sufficiently with the crowds, Sally slipped into a phone booth, dialled and drummed her fingers.

'Mr Winterton?' He was there at last. 'If I tell you that I'm at Heathrow Airport on my way to New Zealand and that I'm hot on the trail of the "tough nut", the "tall, broad and handsome" you-know-who, will you give me a job on the *Star and Journal*?'

Derek Winterton appeared to be robbed of breath. 'Tell me more,' he managed.

So Sally obliged, filling him in on the details, but leaving out the episode of Henni Curzon and the temporary 'engagement'. After all, the whole thing was meaningless, lasting only a few minutes from beginning to end.

'I could send in regular reports, you know, snippets of gossip, like his attitude to the female sex, the love, if any, in his life, what he thinks of fellow writers, not to mention critics. Well,' she finished eagerly, 'do I get the job?'

The long pause had her worried. At last he asked in a world-weary tone, 'What's the guy's destination?'

A valid point, Sally, feeling small, had to admit. 'I don't know, but——'

'So how the blazes,' his voice exploded in her ear, 'can you keep on his trail if he's going east or west and you're going south? Trust an ex-schoolmarm to forget the basics, the facts of air travelling life!'

If she told him this was her first real venture into the unknown, his comments would no doubt break the sound barrier.

'Sorry, Sally, nice try,' she heard him sigh long-sufferingly, 'but better luck next time. And do me a favour, dear. Don't ring me, I'll ring you. Understand?'

Sally understood only too well. She shouldered her bag, visited the ladies' cloakroom and trailed back to the table at which, to her surprise, Max Mackenzie still sat.

He glanced at her and stood, pulling out her chair. 'Tough nut' he might be, Sally thought, but she had to give him full marks for good manners. And, she thought, shouldn't she add thoughtfulness and consideration?

'OK?' he asked, eyeing her narrowly.

He had noticed a change in her! She had to put him off the scent. Managing a smile, she answered, 'A bit tired, not to say worried——'

'About your lost property? So,' he pushed out of the way the bowl containing sweeteners and sugar packets, 'let's figure out what to do about it.'

'It's—it's good of you to bother. After all, it's not your problem.'

A shrug disposed carelessly of her gratitude.

'My main luggage has been checked in,' she told him.

'Another backpack? Like that but larger?'

'Much larger.'

'Hm.' His glance flicked over her. He seemed, among other things, to be endeavouring to assess how her slender frame and delicate air could possibly bear the punishing weight that she, like so many young women in her peer group, roving the world as their mothers when younger had never dreamed of doing, intended inflicting on her body.

'Message for Miss Dearlove,' came over the public address system, *'Miss Sarah Dearlove. Would she please report to the Lost Property office...'*

'My airline bag!' Sally exclaimed, bright-eyed, jumping up. 'Oh, Mr Mackenzie, they've found it. They must have!'

He was behind her at the counter as the bag was handed over, pointing out where she should sign the paper passed to her. As they moved away, her eyes shone into those of her companion.

'I could hug y—— Sorry,' she laughed, 'no, I couldn't.'

'Why not?' he took her up with a smile. 'I blatantly used you earlier for my own ends.' He held out his arms. 'Use me.'

'Oh!' She was so happy to have her lost bag returned to her she could not restrain her impulse, and threw her arms around his ribs, pressing her cheek against his chest, then lifting it and releasing him. 'Thanks. Thanks, Max—for everything.'

'Thank *you*, Sarah,' he joked with a faintly mocking bow, his eyes flashing a very male message which was gone in less than a fraction of a second.

'Sally,' she pointed out after a slightly breathless pause.

'OK, Sally, let's find a seat.' She trailed after him, although she didn't know why, the rediscovered bag firmly in her grip.

For a long moment he regarded her, his glance enigmatic, slanting down, curiously speculative. Sally, surprised by her thoughts—after all, why should she want to please this man, because once their flights had been called, she would never see him again?—wished fervently that, on visiting the ladies' rest-room, she had applied a little powder and tamed her hair into a tidy tail.

'So it was an accident,' he said in a voice which implied that he was still not completely convinced, 'that you fell at my feet? And you're not a member of that perishing fan club?'

'I assure you I'm not. I saw a spare chair, made a beeline,' she smiled, 'for the chair, not you.'

He smiled too, but wryly. 'Thanks for that truly ego-boosting compliment! Point taken. Er—what is Miss Dearlove's destination?'

'Down Under.'

His eyebrows shot up. 'Australia?'

'No, New Zealand. To start with, anyway. You?' she ventured.

'New Zealand.'

'Snap! Truly?'

'Truly,' was his amused reply.

Her eyes lit up. If only she'd known that when she called Derek Winterton! He might even have *offered* her that job, instead of her having to plead for it.

So Max Mackenzie was going her way. Her heart did a frenzied dance of celebration—until reason rushed in and slowed it to a halt.

This man whose skill as a writer of political thrillers had made his name known around the world, and Sarah Dearlove, obscure ex-teacher and would-be journalist, a species he was alleged to hate anyway—why should they meet again on the soil of that distant land?

And remember, her common sense lectured, he's either going hotel-hopping or visiting relatives, whereas you— well, it'll be one youth hostel after another, won't it?

'How many breaking male hearts are you leaving behind?'

She glanced at him quickly, catching a curious expression flickering across his eyes. 'Boyfriends, I suppose you mean? Well...there's Gerald. He didn't want me to go.'

'He wouldn't come with you?'

Sally made a face. 'He's strictly a home bird. Not even an armchair traveller.'

Max sat, legs crossed, head reflectively back, seemingly watching passers-by. 'You'll be visiting relatives?' he queried. 'Or friends of the family?'

She shook her head. 'I want to see the country, that's why I'm going.'

'Mr Mackenzie.' The young man who appeared in front of them held a reporter's notebook, pencil poised. His glance skimmed Sally, registering faint surprise, making her look down at herself and wonder what had caused it. She was certain she heard Max grind his teeth. He seemed master of the art of undercover comments.

'So what if I am?' he said in a bored tone.

'Mart Billing, *Chronicle Weekly*. It's come to our— er—ears—well, mine—telephone message from your fan club——'

'Good grief,' muttered Max, plainly annoyed, 'that lot need their wings clipped!'

'If it was confidential,' Sally took the liberty of pointing out quietly, 'you should have told Henni Curzon so.'

'Don't give me a *lesson*, Miss Dearlove,' he returned through gritted teeth, 'on promotional ethics, nor personal publicity, where fan clubs and the Press are concerned.'

'—that,' Mart Billing pressed on, disregarding his interviewee's murmured comments, 'you've got yourself a——' again his eyes swung to Sally, his long and faintly greasy hair swinging '—a——'

'Yes?' The challenge in Sally's voice plainly took him aback. 'A——' An over-sweet smile illuminated her face. 'A what, Mr Billing?'

'A *lady* in your life, sir,' was the half-strangled answer. 'A fiancée,' he elaborated, glancing at Sally like someone afraid that a pet dog might up and bite him, 'a wife-to-be? Could you confirm, Mr Mackenzie?'

Sally's swift glance at her companion, with its sudden lack of assurance and the question it held, did not miss the reporter's trained eye.

'I take it your—er——' with another apprehensive look in Sally's direction, 'your fiancée is elsewhere?'

Max's arms folded dauntingly. 'Why not ask the lady at my side?'

Mart Billing did a double-take, noting with a reporter's knack for detail the shiny areas on Sally's jacket indicating wear, her worn-to-fraying jeans, her neat but well-washed blouse. 'This—*this* lady?'

Nobody, she wanted to say, would surely dress in their best when travelling tourist class in a jumbo jet? And anyway, her 'best' had been bought some years ago, before her father had been taken ill and before she had had to use her none-too-generous monthly salary to keep not only herself, but her impecunious parents too.

Max, responding to the reporter's somewhat tactless reaction, affected to look worried and glanced about him. 'For God's sake, you're not trying to tell me there's *another* woman who's claiming that position in my life? In this lawsuit-crazy world, a man can't be too careful.'

Sally laughed, then sobered. It was all very well, she thought, for Max Mackenzie to play with representatives of the Press. He was fireproof, a personality, a celebrated writer. Why didn't he help her out?

She turned a reproachful, snappy glance on him. He began to smile at the fire in her eyes, but his amusement faded. Had he, she wondered, as a concerned frown took its place, traced in her expression something of her thoughts?

This man, she mused, is a wonderful guy. Some day, some lucky woman... Not only did he have looks, presence and brains, he was compassionate too.

The reporter turned to her, taking Max Mackenzie at his word. 'Miss—er——'

'Dearlove,' she supplied, 'Sarah Dearlove.'

His reaction was immediate and expected. '*Dearlove?* You did say——'

'Dearlove.' Sally proceeded to spell it, slowly and with exaggerated patience.

The reporter nodded, waiting for more. When none came, he prompted, '*You're* Mr Mackenzie's fiancée?'

Sally's better judgement advised her to simulate mystery. After all, it was not her place to perpetuate a total falsehood on Maximilian Mackenzie's behalf. With a shy glance at Max—which was not completely feigned—she put a finger to her lips.

'No comment,' she replied, half turning away, thus hoping to terminate the interview.

'Tell your reading public,' Max remarked, placing his arm around Sally's shoulders, 'that I consider myself unbelievably lucky to have found such a wonderful lady with whom to share my life.'

That same 'wonderful lady' turned her head, smiling at him, moving closer and playing it his way, glad to follow the lead he was finally giving. He caught at her chin and placed his mouth on hers, his hands moving under her arms, impelling her towards him.

The kiss that had started lightly somehow took off, deepening alarmingly and bringing a flush to Sally's cheeks and a thundering in her ears that had no connection at all with the constant roar of aircraft taking to the skies overhead.

In a subtle way, Max had changed too, his arm muscles hardening, his thighs so taut against her own that her nerve-ends tingled, sounding a thousand alarms inside her head.

When he let her go, she stared into his eyes. If this was Max Mackenzie play-acting, what was he like when playing for real? A light flashed behind them. Pitched back into an unwelcome awareness of the everyday world, Sally pulled away angrily.

'For goodness' sake,' she exclaimed over her shoulder, disentangling herself from Max's hold, 'reporter or not, you've no right to invade anyone's privacy, whether they're famous like Mr Mackenzie here, or a complete unknown like me!'

'You won't be unknown for much longer,' Mart Billing muttered. 'Thanks a lot,' he said aloud, pocketing his camera. 'OK, that ties it up nicely.' He disappeared into the crowd.

A small, strained silence followed as Sally busied herself with her bags. There was an irritation inside her at the turn of events. Why was Max Mackenzie so silent? If he had wanted to deny the assumed connection between them, why had he kissed her with such surprising feeling? He had only to use all the right words to that reporter, and the story about them would have been a non-starter.

Besides, it wasn't her fault that their paths had crossed... but it was! So was he waiting for an apology? If so, she guessed she owed it to him, having got him so involved in her affairs.

Looking up, she began, 'I'm sorry about——'

'Don't apologise.' He was looking down at her, and although his eyes were expressionless, she was sure his thoughts were working overtime, angry about her appearance in his life but being too gentlemanly to say so.

'I did try to give you a way out of the pretence,' she added in her own defence.

'So you did.' As a comment, being spoken in an entirely neutral tone, it told her nothing.

She glanced at the computer screen, searching for her flight number and any information there might be about it.

'I'll get out of your life and leave you in peace, Mr Mackenzie,' she told him. 'Thanks for—for all your help. I'm really sorry to have troubled you. And to have messed up your clothes.' She put out a hand, but he did not meet it with his.

'Hadn't you better look in your airline bag and make sure nothing's gone?' he queried.

Confused by his distant manner after the explosive contact of their lips and bodies, she said, 'Oh, I—I suppose I should. I'm new to all this. I guess I automatically trust people.' She sat down, unzipping the bag and searching its contents. 'My travellers' cheques are in my personal bag, but the currency I drew out isn't there, so I must have put it in this one. That's strange,' she frowned, keeping her panic in check, 'there's no sign...'

She went back to searching her shoulder-bag. As the seconds ticked by, her hands grew moist, her teeth mauling her lower lip. 'Not there either. Whoever found the bag must have taken it. Oh, no,' she groaned, 'not another calamity!' Shimmering eyes lifted to his. 'It's just not my day, is it? Not my—my holiday either.' She shook her head while her fingers went on vainly searching. 'And I've waited so long for this too.'

'No more money in the kitty? You're skint?'

'Cleaned out. A bit of spending money in travellers' cheques, that's all. Poverty-stricken, that's me.' She smiled bravely, dashed at one or two errant tears, then made a self-disparaging face.

'You can't mean it?' He sought in his pocket and produced a handkerchief, handing it to her.

Taking it, she dabbed at her damp cheeks and handed the soft white square back to him. 'Thanks a lot. The story of my life,' she shrugged, attempting to dismiss the subject lightly, 'it's a long one.'

'Too long to tell me?'

She nodded and gritted her teeth as she faced the inevitable consequence of her loss.

'Any ideas about what I can do to get my backpack off the plane, Mr Mackenzie?' she asked.

'There may be ways. We could make enquiries.'

'We', he'd said. Which meant he wasn't contemplating deserting her—yet. The thought was infinitely comforting.

'But,' his glance rested on her reflectively, 'it might not be necessary. It depends on you. I can let you have the necessary cash to see you through your holiday.'

'You mean—lend it to me?'

He answered with another question. 'How much have you lost?'

She told him. 'Not sufficient to cover the time I intended being there, but I'd hoped to work now and then and pay my way like that. The reason I wanted to make this trip,' she felt an explanation was needed as to why she had undertaken the journey, 'was partly a personal one. When my grandfather—my late grandfather,' she paused, recalling the warm, if distant, memories of the white-haired, benevolent man she had loved in her childhood, 'was in his teens many years ago, he travelled to New Zealand. By ship, of course—no jumbos then. He stayed for five years and liked it so much he nearly didn't come back.'

'So it's a sentimental journey?'

'I suppose it is.' She frowned. 'Well, it was.' A sigh jerked unevenly from her, then she smiled a little wanly. 'I can't take money from you, Mr Mackenzie, but thank you for offering it.'

'Look, I——'

'It's no use, I could never pay it back. It took all my savings to pay for my return ticket, plus the bit extra I've now lost. And that's the truth, whether you believe me or not.'

'Oh, I believe you,' he averred. 'Why should I not?'

A voice came over the public address system, urging those who were on the flight number which Sally recognised as hers to proceed to the appropriately numbered gate prior to boarding.

Panic sharpened her gaze as she stared at Max Mackenzie. 'My luggage—I can't go home without that! It's on that plane. It's got all my—well, almost all my worldly goods in it. What can I——?'

'You've got your ticket?' he asked sharply. 'OK. As for ready cash, you can—and you will—borrow, yes, I said borrow, from me.' He picked up his own hand luggage, seizing Sally's with his other hand, which meant that she had no option but to follow him.

He handed her the airline bag as they went through Security. He was directed to another channel and she was delayed by the person in front of her. By the time she was through, Max had gone. A group was being directed on to the aircraft.

'Club class passengers, lucky beggars,' she heard someone say. Tall as Max was, Sally was able to identify him as he moved in the line which was boarding the plane in advance of the crowd. Of course, she was one of that 'crowd'.

Her heart unaccountably dived. He had gone, the man who, for the past hour or so, had come to resemble a rock to which she had been clinging just above a tempestuous sea. She felt she had lost a friend.

He had promised her financial help, but people, even friends, often made promises they had no intention of keeping. But it wasn't only that, she admitted to herself, that was making her feel she had suffered a heart-shaking loss.

It was the man himself she missed, his self-confidence, his proud bearing, his air of reliability; his keen eyes, the way he did something to her—that second kiss he had given her, to impress the reporter though it had been, had left its mark on her lips, and her innermost feelings. There had been a magnetic quality about him which deep down she had found almost irresistible.

Already, she realised, she was thinking about him in the past tense. Swept along by the crowd, she found herself boarding the plane and finding her seat, which adjoined the gangway. Having stowed her hand luggage, she gazed around, wondering where Max was.

At least, she consoled herself, he's on this plane somewhere. But being the well-known personality that he was, he would already have put her to the back of his mind and she would probably never see him again.

'Miss Dearlove.' She opened her eyes at the softly spoken sound of her name. Her gaze widened at the sight of the man who had spoken it. Her heart began to throb louder than the plane's engines. It couldn't be a dream, because she hadn't been asleep.

'I'm sorry if I——' he began.

She shook her head. 'I was thinking, that's all.'

He bent down, his hand on the arm of her seat. She caught the faint and pleasant scent of him, noticed the way his eyebrows arched as they tapered slightly away; the faint shadow across his upper lip, the high cheekbones, the curved sweep of his jaw. And she liked—yes, she liked what she saw so much it almost hurt.

He looked around. It was as well, she reflected, that he couldn't read her thoughts! 'You're in the smoking area. Do you smoke? No? The man beside me does, but to his annoyance, by mistake his seat's for non-smokers He tried to change it but couldn't. I told him I'd have a word with you on his behalf. Would you have any objection to swapping your seat for his?'

'I—I'd love to help him, but I——' It pained her to have to keep repeating it. 'I couldn't afford——'

'No finance involved—a straight swap. You'd both benefit from the move.'

Sally had the greatest difficulty in preventing herself from dancing the Highland fling in the gangway. Yes, please! she wanted to cry. 'No, I—I wouldn't mind,' she said aloud, pleased with her own show of restraint.

Max opened the overhead locker and extracted her airline bag, a piece of luggage which Sally reminded herself he knew only too well, and invited her to follow.

With the 'smoking' passenger's 'eternal gratitude', as he called it, ringing in her ears, Sally settled herself, much more comfortably, and secretly delightedly, beside the man she had been so certain she would never see again.

'OK?' he asked, and as she nodded, he pulled his newspaper, his orange juice-stained newspaper, from the pocket of the seat in front and proceeded to read it.

No man, she thought, stealing a glance at his unaware profile, should have eyelashes as long as his, nor a face so arresting and full of character.

'If you don't mind my mentioning it,' she commented a little hesitantly, 'that stain on your shirt—it seems to have gone. Did you manage to remove it?'

'One observant lady,' was his wry reply. 'I bought a new shirt in Duty Free when you disappeared to powder your nose. The soiled one's in my bag.'

'Please let me pay for your new shirt,' she began, then frowned in confusion as she realised, impoverished as her financial loss had made her, what a futile offer it was.

Comprehending at once, he said with a dry smile, 'I appreciate the offer, but even if you had the money, do you really think I'd have accepted?'

Busying herself with opening her bag, Sally attempted to control the *frissons* of excitement which ran in circles around her shoulder as his upraised arm holding the newspaper pressed ever so slightly against it.

She withdrew a compact, flipping open the lid and pausing in the act of lifting the powder puff to her nose. That part of her heart-shaped face was unrepentantly shiny, although that fact, she supposed modestly, did not detract from its overall pleasantness.

Her lips, full and inviting, were still a little taut, which together with a fine layer of moisture just above them told of the effect which the day's stresses and strains had had on her equilibrium. What troubled her most was that she still did not know how she was going to pay her way in the days that lay immediately ahead.

Her hair, she discovered, was a mess, although she had had it shortened to jaw-length for easy management while she was away. Later, she would comb it; not now, with Max Mackenzie beside her, ready, no doubt, to raise a sardonic eyebrow at such a feminine act of vanity, as she was certain he would regard it.

'Finished?' He was looking at her askance and folding away his paper. There was a hint of amusement in his tone.

'Yes, thank you. Well, not really,' she amended, 'but——'

'You look fine to me. Tell me,' he pushed his newspaper away, 'what's your job?'

'I'm—I *was* a teacher. Of English. To teenagers.' He nodded and she went on a little dreamily, 'One day, I looked out of the classroom window and thought, There must be more to life than this. There's a whole world out there waiting to be explored.'

'So you quit?'

'The feeling of freedom when I did!'

'You'd decided to follow in your grandfather's footsteps?'

She nodded. 'I looked out his memoirs—they were never published. His descriptions were so good, I said to myself, that's where I'll go—I'll travel those twelve thousand miles and see what my grandad saw all those years ago.'

'It will be very different now,' he warned.

'That's what I want to find out.' She looked at him with curiosity. 'What is it that's calling you across the world? Is your family there, which is why so many people seem to make this journey?' His hesitation conveyed to her that he was reluctant to explain. 'Don't tell me, Mr Mackenzie. It's none of my business.'

She made to extract the airline magazine, but his hand on hers stopped her. She liked the touch of him, it brought back the sensation that his kisses had caused within her.

Her assumption that he regarded her question as impertinent was wrong. 'Yes, I have family living here and there, North Island and the South too. But that isn't my chief reason for going.' Pushing aside his paper, he stretched out his legs, folded his arms and put back his head. For the first time since she had met him, Sally saw him relaxed and off guard, and as such, in her eyes, much less formidable.

'You know by now that I'm a writer? Yes,' drily as she nodded, 'as you witnessed one of my fans almost literally flinging herself at me, that fact could hardly have escaped your notice.'

I like the way he smiles, Sally thought, glad beyond words that fate had taken a hand in rearranging the seating so that she now found herself beside him.

'Was the book Henni Curzon wanted you to autograph your latest?' she asked, risking a reproof for daring to mention the subject.

'It was,' he answered equably, 'which is one of the reasons why I'm making this journey—touring the country to promote the book, seeing members of my family at the same time. Now, enough about me. I promised you financial help. If I give you a cheque in New Zealand dollars for the amount you've lost...'

Sally shook her head. 'I told you, Mr Mackenzie, I could never pay it back.'

'You're on this plane, flying to the other side of the world,' he said, eyes closed, arms folded, 'so tell me, Sally, if I accept that statement and withdraw my offer, what will you do for money? No one will accommodate you or sell you goods of whatever description in return for IOUs or mere promises to pay.'

'The answer is,' Sally replied, 'I—I simply don't know. I don't possess any credit cards, simply because I knew I couldn't pay when the accounts arrived. And I refuse on principle to let my debts mount up.'

He nodded without stirring from his semi-somnolent position. He was silent for so long, Sally's spirits began to submerge without trace.

'Thanks,' she added with a sigh, 'for your kindness in offering to come to my rescue. But I honestly don't know of any way, not in the foreseeable future, that is, or in the future beyond that, that I'd be able to reimburse you.'

'I could make the amount, whatever it might be, a gift.'

'You mean,' Sally queried, aghast, 'you'd be *giving* me the money?' She shook her head so fiercely her hair swung wide and made sweeping contact with his face.

Removing the strands that still clung lovingly to his jacket, Max nodded. A smile flickered across his expressive mouth, but whether or not it was in amusement at being stroked by her tresses or at her horrified tone, she could not tell.

'You're saying no?' His mouth was twitching again.

'Definitely I'm saying no. But thank you. Very much.'

'A rarity, a jewel to treasure,' he murmured sardonically, 'a woman who refuses money when it's offered *gratis*.' Another long pause, and Sally began to wonder if he was asleep. Consequently, she jumped when he opened his eyes and turned his head against the headrest. 'We'll make it a long-term loan, then. Interest-free, no time limit.'

'It's no use, Mr Mackenzie,' Sally repeated, desperate for him to understand. 'I told you, I would never be able to——'

'Repay me? There is a way.' He straightened and looked fully at her. 'You need a job. On my travels I shall need an assistant. A young woman acquaintance of my aunt's had agreed to fill that post during my stay in New Zealand, but she's unable to keep her promise. I need—urgently need—a replacement for her. I'm asking you, Miss Dearlove, to be that replacement.'

CHAPTER THREE

SALLY woke to the sound of a telephone ringing in someone else's room. The long flight, the hustle at the airport, the drive to the city in a large car that had been awaiting Maximilian Mackenzie's arrival—they all sprang to mind as she focused on the strange surroundings and tried to shake off her drowsiness.

The dark-eyed, dusky-skinned young woman who had met them and warmly shaken Max's hand appeared puzzled to discover that he was not alone.

'Keri Okiru,' she announced. 'Your publisher's Auckland rep. Remember me?' Max assured her that he did. 'Welcome back, Mr Mackenzie,' she said with a bright smile. She transferred that smile to Sally. 'Head office in London said you'd be alone, but——' Her hand extended to Sally, the welcome just as warm.

'This is Sarah Dearlove,' Max introduced. 'She's agreed to act as my assistant, filling the gap left by Janey Petts.'

Keri nodded, pushing back her thick, night-dark hair. 'We had someone lined up to take her place, but it seems you've found a substitute for yourself. Delighted to meet you, Miss Dearlove.'

'Make it Sally, *please*,' Sally prompted. 'I'm an informal kind of person, and Sarah doesn't go with me, if you know what I mean.'

Keri had laughed, laughing again when Sally had proceeded to explain just how 'informal' her introduction to Max Mackenzie had been.

Sally rolled on to her side and felt like sleeping some more, but knew that if she didn't resist the urge, it would take her body much longer to recover from jet lag, and her inner clock to adjust to the time change. Her thoughts drifted back to the moment when Max had offered her the job as his assistant.

'I'll be travelling,' he had said, 'which means that you would be able to see the country just as you'd planned. My itinerary will involve meeting people, giving talks, attending signing sessions. The salary that goes with the job,' he had informed her, 'will be easily sufficient to see you through your travels in this country, maybe even help you to build up a reserve for whatever purpose you might have in mind. So, Miss Dearlove,' he had half twisted in his seat, 'how about it?'

Sally had opened her mouth to voice her uncertainty, her doubts about her ability to fulfil such a role when he declared, 'I never take "no". When you know me better, you'll realise that I get my way no matter what.'

When she knew him better? 'But you don't understand,' she protested. 'I was trained as a teacher, not—— '

'Can you type? You can? Then what's the problem?'

'Trained,' she enlarged, 'as an independent thinker, and, I hope, to awaken young minds to do likewise. I wasn't trained to take orders unquestioningly as a good secretary should.'

'You're making excuses and putting up barriers which have little or no relevance to the subject in question. Look,' he shifted in his seat and frowned down at her, 'I wouldn't know what to do with a secretary, even if she obligingly presented herself, notepad in hand. Except...'

His eyes had held a faintly sensual glint as he looked her over, dishevelled as she was. 'I don't dictate my work,' he went on, plainly having decided to keep his thoughts to himself, 'I write in longhand. I'm a creative writer, not a businessman. An assistant is what I want, and an assistant is what I asked you to be.'

'It's not a sinecure? You haven't made it up to help me? You really do need——?'

'As I explained,' he interrupted with forced patience, 'there *is* a job and I really do need. So?'

'I'll—I'll have a try. But——'

'No buts.' His hand came out. 'We'll shake on it.'

Sally had put hers into his, and had felt a shiver run through her nervous system as the 'shake' had turned curiously into a softly stroking motion. His eyes had smiled into hers, and it felt as if the aircraft had turned over in the very same way as her heart had been doing at exactly that moment.

Against her will, Sally began to drift back to semiconsciousness when an abrupt knock on the door caused her legs to swing out, her hand to grab a bedcover and wrap it round her. She cursed the fact that, having been so weary on arrival, she had omitted to take a single item of clothing from her baggage.

Max was standing in the corridor, envelope in hand. He looked her over, smiled slightly at her curious appearance, wrapped around as she was, then asked with raised eyebrows, 'May I come in?'

'I'm not dressed for visitors,' she said uncertainly, but opened the door to allow him to enter, trailing her voluminous covering across to the bed and sinking on to it.

'The world——' she peered through the uncombed wisps of her dark brown hair '—is not in its right place. All these hours ahead of what I'm used to, not to mention my inner being,' she sighed, 'I'm completely disorientated.'

'Believe me, it will pass.' He looked around. 'Do you like this room? Any complaints?'

'Yes, and no, in that order. How could I complain? I mean, I left home with the intention of staying at youth hostels because that was all I would have been able to afford. Yet here I am…all this luxury! Thank you again for it.'

Max returned her smile, holding out the envelope. 'An advance on salary.' He held up his hand. 'No objections. As my assistant, you'll be moving in circles you couldn't possibly have imagined when you packed for your journey.' He took her hand, placing the envelope on her palm. 'For a couple of new outfits, and whatever else takes your fancy.'

'I——' Sally's shoulders lifted and fell. 'I guess I have no alternative. You're right about my clothes. Strictly utilitarian, easy to wash, non-iron. It's——' she looked up at him, looked away, wondering if she should go on, deciding she had to now '—it's years since I've been able to buy something nice for myself.'

He seemed to be waiting for more, but she couldn't oblige. It was locked inside her and she had mislaid the key. She looked at him again. Until that moment, she had sat beside him, stood at his side, walked along with him. Now he stood apart from her, tall, broad-shouldered, lean and incredibly attractive and she realised she was seeing him objectively for the first time.

His suit was impeccably cut, his plain red tie a tasteful contrast against the darkness of the suit's fabric. In his face was the merest hint of arrogance. There were lines too, deep grooves bracketing his jawline, etched pleats between his brows, chin thrusting uncompromisingly forward. His mouth told the world quite plainly that it brooked no nonsense from anyone, while in his eyes, intensely blue, was a keen intelligence, plus a hint of cynicism fighting for supremacy with an unmistakable brush-stroke of compassion.

Yet she could see now that beyond that sympathy and desire to help which she had encountered as a result of her first accident-prone meeting with him was an iron strength, a steeliness that, like a high brick wall, was intended to keep out all comers, except perhaps a fortunate few who were allowed access to the heart and soul of him.

'What's the verdict, teacher?' he asked, his lips faintly curved. 'Bottom of the class, Mackenzie, for integrity and honesty?'

Sally laughed, an action that served to ease the tension which, strangely, had manifested itself between them. Her heart did a cartwheel, that strange antic that seemed to overtake it whenever he was near.

'I'll—er—give you your exam results at the end of term,' she returned, taking his cue. 'You can take your revenge by summing me up, if you like. As a writer, of course,' slanting him an impudent glance, 'analysing my character, taking me apart, then putting me together again to fit better into your plot.'

'Yours, lady,' he advanced a threatening step or two, but still keeping his distance, 'would be too elusive, too complex a personality for me ever to contemplate unravelling.'

'You'd be afraid of finding one piece of my character left over when you've put me together again?' He laughed. 'Do you really know all this on the short acquaintance that ours has been?'

'Oh, yes, I know,' he replied mysteriously. 'And yet——' his eyes lingered on her upturned face '—I don't know. There's something that keeps me guessing...'

His eyes had narrowed, and a shiver took hold of her beneath the folds of the cover swathed around her. He didn't know—he hadn't guessed, had he?—about her wish to become a journalist, one of that breed he was alleged to dislike so much? If he ever discovered it, what would he say? More important, what would he do? Send her packing?

She needn't worry on that score, Sally assured herself. Hadn't the editor of the *Star and Journal* given her the classic brush-off, Don't ring me, I'll ring you? She looked at the cheque in her hand. It was for a large amount, even when the New Zealand dollars were divided to give the answer in the currency she was accustomed to.

'Thank you for this, Mr Mackenzie. I——'

'Max.'

She looked up at him again, aware that a curious intimacy had crept in. 'Max,' she whispered, finding her mouth go curiously dry at the shadowed look in his eyes. 'I——' She endeavoured to moisten her lips. 'I'll use this to buy some outfits suitable for the job as assistant to the celebrated Max Mackenzie which he was kind enough to offer me.'

'One thing I am not, as you will learn, is kind,' he told her.

Sally smiled. 'Have it your way, Mr Mackenzie—I mean Max.'

'I usually do, Miss Dearlove.' He smiled. 'I mean Sally.' He became brisk, looking at his watch. 'One hour to dinner.' Which explained his formal suit. 'Join me for drinks, will you, in the lounge in, say, half an hour.'

She looked at the bundle that was her backpack, still securely fastened. 'I'm afraid I can't match your mode of dress,' she told him. 'Not yet, anyway, not until I've been to the shops.'

His hand moved dismissively at her statement.

Looking for him as she entered the lounge, Sally saw Keri Okiru first. She was seated on a settee beside Max, her eyes bright and merry, laughing at something he had said. As Sally approached, Max rose, and Keri stood also, gesturing to her that she should take her place.

'No, please,' Sally protested, 'I'll just——'

'I'm off, anyway,' said Keri. 'Max,' he rose again, 'I'm so annoyed that my annual leave coincides with your visit here, but I've given you your itinerary, and with Sally's help, I'm sure you'll be OK.' As their hands clasped, Keri gave his cheek a farewell kiss, which he returned. Then she smiled. 'If I weren't in such a rush, I'd demonstrate the traditional Maori greeting—touching noses—for Sally's benefit. Bye.'

'People like Keri,' Sally said after a moment, reaching for the drink that Max had offered her, 'leave a warm feeling in your heart. I suppose you've met her before?'

'A number of times. On my more recent visits, she's been at the airport to meet me.' He finished his drink, then handed Sally the menu. 'I was born here.'

'So you're a New Zealander? I would never have guessed. But now you've told me, I can detect—just— the faintest intonation in your accent.'

He laughed. 'So it hasn't all been ironed out by the years I've spent in Britain?'

'Fortunately, no,' Sally answered, adding with a shy smile, 'I rather like it.' She looked around, then down at the simple white blouse and floral cotton skirt she was wearing. 'I'm glad to see that casual dress is in over here.'

'It is, and,' Max leaned back cornerwise against the sofa arm, his sideways glance taking in her sandalled feet and neat outfit, 'casual, informal or whatever, you look fine to me.'

I'd like to bet, Sally thought, that your ex-fiancée— didn't Derek Winterton say her name was Francine Something?—dressed like a model? And I also bet, she added to herself, you loved it. 'Thanks for that boost to my confidence,' she said aloud.

'Tomorrow is free,' he told her over dinner, 'to allow for jet-lag recovery.' He slid a list from his jacket pocket. 'Next day, a signing at the main bookshop, then a 'meet-the-fans' session, followed by couple of talks. We leave

Auckland—hired car, I drive—at the end of the week.'
He pocketed the itinerary. 'Should be some time there
for sightseeing.'

'Yes, please!' Sally clasped her hands, her face
glowing, at which point she was overtaken by a shaking
yawn which left her eyes watering with exhaustion. 'Max,
I'm so sorry...'

He rose. 'Jet-lag signals, loud and clear. I'll show you
to your room.'

He took her key, opening the door and using his
powerful shoulder to prevent its strong spring from
swinging it shut.

'Tomorrow, Max,' Sally looked up at him, 'could I
roam the city and look for an outfit or two?'

'Do whatever you want,' he answered. 'Are you the
kind of lady who doesn't like a male tagging along?'

Sally smiled. 'If that male,' she answered, her heart
lifting, 'is offering his services as a guide, then the answer
to your question is no, I'm not.'

'Fine. I rise early, take a brisk walk, write a bit, then
have breakfast. You?'

'I get up when the alarm tells me, do a few exercises,
swallow some food and gather my notes for the day.
Then I go to school—to teach.'

'Ah.' He smiled, the creases around his mouth
deepening. 'In the circumstances, you'll need to alter
your schedule here and there, don't you think? That was
then; this is now. You've changed your occupation.'

'You're right. Perhaps I'd better restate that.' Sally
counted on her fingers. 'Alarm, exercises, eat—then I'll
be at your beck and call.'

His eyelids drooped slightly as he seemed deliberately
to read more into her words than had been intended.
The moment passed and Sally, flushing a little, made a
mental note to remember how swiftly he seemed to re-

spond to sensual signals, unintentional though they might be.

'Goodnight, Max,' she said, taking the weight of the door from his shoulder. 'It's been a long, long day. Thanks for everything. And I do hope you won't regret offering me the job as your assistant.'

'You might be the one to have regrets,' he said, turning to go. 'I might turn out to be a fiend.'

'Workwise, maybe, maybe not, but as a person.' Sally gave a definite shake of the head. 'Oh, no!'

'Don't bet on it,' was his answer as he strode away.

The day dawned hot and brilliantly sunny, and it passed in a whirl of shopping and sightseeing.

Arriving back at the hotel tired but happy, Sally left Max, telling him she intended trying on her purchases, then showering before changing for dinner.

Having discovered a shop which catered for people with her particular taste in clothes, she had bought two or three outfits that could be mixed and matched to suit, she hoped, most of Max's social commitments. While she made her choice, he had left her to call in on the Auckland offices of his publishers.

Returning for her an hour later, he had produced the tickets he had bought for a cruise around Waitemata Harbour. After coffee at a café at the harbour front, where birds hopped around, avidly pecking the crumbs on and around the tables, they had strolled to the landing stage and waited for the cruise boat to arrive.

Sharing a bench with Max in the hot sun, Sally had listened to the foreign languages being spoken all around them.

Fascinated, she had watched a ferryboat plying back and forth to the northern part of the city, while canoers arrowed in all directions and gulls wheeled and glided

on the stiff breeze, squawking shrilly to the music from
loudspeakers that followed them through the air.

Now, taking a bath instead of the shower she had
mentioned, Sally lay back and closed her eyes, living
again the pleasures of the harbour cruise.

After coffee on board, she had stood at the ship's rail,
the wind lifting her hair and filling her lungs, and revelled in the fact that she had at last broken free of her
old life and had made it to the other side of the world.

In the past, the parameters of her own world, through
her financial struggles to help her parents...had been
so limited and confined that she had never allowed
herself even to look at a travel brochure, let alone consider taking an overseas holiday.

All around, yachts, some towing small boats, had cut
their way through the water, their brightly coloured sails
billowing. Motor-boats, wallowing in the wash the tour
cruiser left behind, had leapt and jumped as if they were
alive. The sea itself was unruffled and blue-green in
colour, while the great span of Auckland Harbour Bridge
came ever nearer.

'Locals call it the "coathanger",' Max had told her,
leaning beside her on the rail, 'because of its shape. The
volume of traffic it carried increased so fast, another
four lanes were added in a skilful piece of "clip-on"
engineering, although not without some technical
troubles.'

He had stared at the yachts and at passing ferryboats,
saying nothing, but seemingly enjoying the sun's warmth
and the blue skies as much as she was. Now and then,
Sally had looked at him to speak her thoughts, but his
silence seemed to have erected a wall around him too
high for her to scale, a wall he had retreated behind to
dwell on his own private thoughts. Something, she
sensed, was troubling him, and she wondered if, despite
his unfailing politeness towards her, he was regretting

her unconventional eruption into his life and her continuing presence there.

Drying herself and brushing her brown hair until it crackled, Sally chose one of the outfits she had bought. Its wrap-around top, with its bracelet-length sleeves, moulded itself to her shape, while the skirt flared gracefully down to her calves.

Raking in a drawer, she found her gold, diamond-shaped locket, one of the few pieces of jewellery she had brought with her. It had been her father's last gift to her, and through long and loving use, its catch had broken.

When Gerald had volunteered to mend it, Sally had gladly accepted. Having carried out the repair, he had surreptitiously inserted a tiny picture of himself cut out from a photograph. Since then Sally had not had the heart to remove it, mainly as a gesture of thanks for his efforts.

As she fixed the locket around her neck, it nestled in the deep V of the bodice. In it she had also placed her mother's address, along with Gerald's and Derek Winterton's phone numbers—not, she thought ruefully, that the latter was any use to her now. 'Don't ring me,' he'd said, and had meant it.

Anyway, Derek would have no idea where she was staying, since she had told him that the only type of accommodation she would be able to afford on her travels was whatever youth hostel could offer a place for a night or two, in whatever part of the world she might find herself.

So, technology or no brilliant, modern technology, communication from him to her was impossible. Which meant, she told herself, that that coveted job on the *Star and Journal*, with or without her uncle's help, was now an impossible dream.

Making her way towards the hotel lounge a little earlier than Max had suggested, Sally wandered along corridors, peering round partly opened doors, discovering conference-rooms and small offices whose entrances bore the words, 'For the use of hotel patrons only'.

Walking past reception, Sally surfaced from the reverie into which she had drifted to hear the words, 'paging Miss Dearlove, paging Miss Sally Dearlove!' echoing through the entrance lobby. Since, Sally decided, there couldn't be another Sally Dearlove in this neck of the woods, she made her way to the reception desk.

'I'm Sally Dearlove,' she told the smiling assistant.

'Phone call for you, Miss Dearlove,' she said.

Of course, Sally thought, it was Max trying to reach her, telling her he would be later down for dinner than he had reckoned. Her composure was shattered when the girl said, 'Long-distance, Miss Dearlove—the UK. Would you like to take it in that little room across there? We'll put you through.'

Her first thought was that her mother might be ill and that her stepfather was contacting her... but how would he know where to find her? How would anyone know?

'Sally? For pity's sake, you've been long enough! You think the *Star and Journal*'s made of money? Twelve thousand miles via satellite and me dashing breakfastless from a warm bed to a cold office to catch you before you go to bed—and you take your time? All the same, you've been a clever little girl. What a brilliant move to insinuate yourself into heart-throb Maximilian Mackenzie's affections by getting him to propose. Congrats. When's the wedding?'

'What,' Sally broke in, almost choking on a gasp, 'are you talking about?'

'It's just got to be true,' said Derek Winterton so loudly that Sally had to hold the receiver away from her ear, 'it's here in the papers.'

Which, Sally thought, was surely just about the most naïve, the most laughable thing a hardened journalist, and a newspaper editor at that, could say.

'What papers? I haven't been in touch with——' Oh, no...Mart Billing of the *Chronicle Weekly*! You won't be unknown for much longer, he'd said.

'There's a photo of you and Mackenzie in a clinch, then there's a report. I quote, "The celebrated and best-selling author and one-time journalist, Maximilian Mackenzie, caught here at Heathrow Airport on his departure for his native New Zealand, finds a *novel* way to announce his latest liaison, his engagement to "complete unknown"—her words, folks—Miss Sarah Dearlove."'

'But,' Sally gasped, 'it's not——'

'There's more,' Derek broke in. 'Listen. He goes on—terrible style, I wouldn't allow it in my paper, but that's the Chronic *Chronicle* for you, 'OK, so she's sweet and lavender-pretty, but has she got something! Cuddly and warm-hearted? You've got it, folks, but turn the heat up a bit, will you? Just look at that snap—wouldn't you say she's...just too hot to handle? Let me tell you, she can stand up for herself. I got an earful from her lovely lips. Is this Maximilian Mackenzie's choice after the failure of his last engagement—to the glamorous and gorgeous Francine Anderley? Did he think it was safer to swing to the opposite end of the female spectrum and choose a jeans-clad, fresh-faced *ingénue*—safer for his reputation and his image? Not to mention...his *heart*?'

Sally swallowed hard, then managed, 'So? Why have you called me?' She was struck by a thought. 'How did you know where I was staying?'

'Simple. Used my contacts. I've got an ex-colleague who moved to a New Zealand paper a couple of years back. I found out through him Mackenzie's NZ publishers and rang them—told them I wanted to do a piece on him in connection with his latest bestseller, and where was he staying, please? Then, hey presto, ask and you'll get, and get what you want, which was you, at the other end.'

'Will you tell me why, Mr Winterton?' demanded Sally.

'Can't you guess? I'm offering you that job you pestered me for. Consider yourself as from now a reporter on contract to the publishers of the *Star and Journal*. As the great man's fiancée, you'll have access to——'

'Thank you, Mr Winterton,' Sally returned levelly, 'for your kind offer, but I've changed my mind. As Max Mackenzie's assistant——'

'Fiancée.'

'*Assistant*, Mr Winterton——'

'Isn't it true, then? You're not his fiancée?'

Sally exhaled a sharp breath and repeated, 'I'm his assistant. That story about my being his fiancée came about by accident, as a direct result of the unwanted attentions at the airport of a devoted fan of his.' Then she remembered Mart Billing's part in it. 'And through that particular member of the Press pestering us.'

'Ah.' Derek was silent for a moment. Then, 'That's good, that's great. It means that as his assistant you can release private info. about him without a qualm.'

Another sigh, sharper this time. 'The answer's still no. I've got standards, even if some sections of the Press haven't.'

He named a sum. 'How's that for a salary?'

It took her breath away. 'It—it's a big, juicy carrot, Mr Winterton, but——'

'OK.' Derek sighed this time. 'Just think about it, that's all I ask. You know my number. But remember there's a hell of a difference timewise between this part of the world and the one you're in at the moment.' He rang off, and Sally was left staring at the receiver.

'Thanks,' she said with a shaky smile to the reception-ist at the desk outside, and walked slowly towards the lounge. So, over there the story was out. The fact that it was a non-story made no difference. It was there in print, and all those who read it would, like Derek Winterton, believe it.

Should she warn Max so that he could issue a denial? She couldn't, she just couldn't! Because if she did, she would need to explain to him how she had come to hear the news—through the editor of a newspaper she had almost begged to join.

It occurred to her that if she were to take up Mr Winterton's offer now and Max Mackenzie were ever to discover her deception, she would find herself bundled out of his life before she could blink, and she would never see him again.

And that, she discovered to her dismay, was begin-ning to matter to her very much indeed.

CHAPTER FOUR

MAX stood as she entered, looking distinguished and handsome in his formal suit. His height and leanness, even without the strong planes of his face, made him superior, in her increasingly partial eyes, in physique and bearing to all the other men around.

As she looked at him, Sally experienced a flip of happiness, mixed with a generous dash of pride—although why, she did not know, because she had no right, since she wasn't truly his fiancée.

Don't think, she lectured herself, that he advanced you that money solely for your benefit. He had his own image in mind, an image he had to cherish through being a well-known and recognisable personality. No one in his position, she was sure, would welcome having every evening as his dinner companion a woman whose clothes were as crumpled and well worn as those that she had pushed into her rucksack in, it seemed to her at that moment, another world, another lifetime.

Now, thanks to his generosity, she had this evening been able to wear a dress that did not let him down. In fact, she had not felt so well dressed for years. Gilt hoops swung from her ears, and her hair sprang softly, framing her oval face and dipping in a sweeping curve just above her shoulders.

As she approached, his attention seemed to be riveted by her appearance. While it lasted, which was scarcely more than a couple of seconds, his concentrated glance unnerved her a little and threatened to upset her new-found poise.

Sally reached him at last and in no time at all he returned to his normal and slightly withdrawn self. She had to face it—there had been surprise, not admiration, in his reaction. This was the first time—it wouldn't have passed his notice—that she had been able to appear before him as anything other than a slightly unkempt, somewhat disorganised backpacker.

None the less, his words of greeting both surprised and worried her. She made a note never to underestimate his powers of observation.

'You look somewhat hassled. Has something happened to upset you?'

So that was why he had been staring at her! And there was I, she thought, persuading myself that I'd successfully hidden the turmoil Derek Winterton's phone call had caused inside me.

'No, no, it—er—hasn't. I'm fine, thanks.'

He came round to her side of the table and helped her into her seat. His impeccable manners still overwhelmed her, and deepened the flush which had, as a result of the phone call, and her pretence that it had never happened, dyed her cheeks.

'Look,' Max sat opposite her, elbows on the table, hands loosely clasped, 'if you want out from my affairs, please tell me. Call the advance on salary I've given you a long-term loan. There's been no contract signed between us. You're as free as a bird to fly unencumbered into the great unknown.'

Her heart seemed to take off, then crash wingless to the ground. 'Is that a polite way of telling me,' she asked over the pages of the menu, 'that you don't want me as your assistant? That you don't think I'll suit? That you've got someone else lined up? Or that it really was a sinecure appointment, produced for my benefit on the spur of the moment, even though you denied it?'

'For God's sake!' He seemed really angry. 'First, no one in their right mind is "polite" in matters of business, and I like to think I'm in my right mind. Second, if I hadn't *wanted* you as my assistant, I wouldn't have given you the job, because it *is* a job, it exists. There's no one else "lined up" for it. And, as far as I can tell from our so far purely surface acquaintance, as an ex-teacher of English, with the ability to type, you would seem ideally suited. Now, what have you chosen to eat?'

'I'm sorry,' she returned, her tone subdued. 'I didn't intend to annoy you. It's just that—well, from that rather disastrous moment of our meeting, you've done all the giving, whereas I——'

'Have no fear, Miss Dearlove——' his eyes detached themselves from the list of dishes they had been perusing and hovered over her, their message unmistakably sensual '—there are ways...and ways...of giving in return. If you get my meaning?'

'No, I don't. If you——' She pushed back her chair.

'What I had in mind, Sarah, was not—quite—what you assume. Now, draw up your chair again, and tell me what you want me to order.'

Towards the end of the meal, Sally sensed that Max's frame of mind had mellowed. Whether it was the effect of the wine he had shared with her, or that his appetite had been indulged and satisfied, she could not be sure. She did realise, however, that she was becoming increasingly attuned to his differing moods.

She realised, also, that she was beginning to like him. No, she reflected with some dismay, it was something more than "liking", something deeper, that involved emotion, plus... In fact, she was beginning to treasure every moment she spent with him... Oh, heavens, stop! she told her thoughts. It was a dead end, wasn't it?

Hadn't he acted towards her, right from the start, as no more than a friend? So what if he'd kissed her? It was good, it was fantastic—crazy ex-fiancée for walking the other way!—but the kiss had only been bestowed to prove a point to that much too inquisitive reporter. So forget it, Sally Dearlove, do you hear?

'Max?'

'Mm?' His glance swung to rest on her and she wished the wall lights were shedding a brighter glow so that she could read the unspoken words in his eyes. As his lips curved in a half-smile, her heart tripped. She righted it with some annoyance. It ought to have known better than to be thrown off balance by a smile from the man who, she had once read, had had a down on women ever since that fiancée of his had absented herself from his life.

'Would you please outline my duties as your assistant?' she asked him.

He sighed with rare good humour. 'You seem determined to make me work!' He eyed the lounge area of the large dining section and rose, inviting her to join him.

Leading the way to a secluded corner some distance from the rotating entrance doors, he waited while Sally seated herself on a sofa, then joined her there, stretching his arm disconcertingly close along the upholstered back.

'This is my routine. Are you listening, Miss Dearlove?' Strong fingers pushed their way through the thickness of her hair, making tormenting contact with her scalp and turning her head his way. His smile, curving his strong mouth and deepening the grooves around it, turned her bones to water. Oh, no, she thought, I'm falling in deeper by the minute!

'I'm listening,' she whispered, her mouth dry.

'You seem,' he commented, those sardonic lips twitching a little, 'to be suffering from a new and serious affliction—mind wandering, I think I'd call it.'

'Sorry about that,' she laughed. If he but knew just where that wayward mind of hers had led her at that moment! 'It's just that—well, part of me is still up there,' she indicated the ceiling, 'sort of suffering from a bad bout of levitation, resting on air and watching events with amazement, unable to believe that the self that's down here is actually on the other side of the world.' And with you, she almost added. He laughed and her shining eyes sought his. 'I just can't believe I've made it, Max, after all those years of longing to break free.'

'What kept you?'

A sigh was jerked from her as she retreated into the past. 'My father's illness, my mother quite unable to cope without my financial and practical help. Then my dad died, and my mother went to pieces.'

'So you had to care for her?'

Sally nodded. 'It took her years to climb out of the shadows she found to hide in in the valley. Then she met someone, a great guy of her own age called Jeff Welling, and she somehow clawed her way back to the top of the emotional slippery slope. Now,' she smiled again, 'my mother's Mrs Edie—Edith—Welling, living in the north of England, and very happy.'

'And all that time, you had to——'

'Try to make ends meet on my not-very-generous teacher's salary.'

'And sometimes those ends wouldn't meet, because they were too far apart?'

'Something like that. I'm not asking for your pity,' Sally added fiercely.

'I'm not giving it. But I understand things a bit better now.'

'My worry about the loss of my money, you mean? My "little girl lost" act at the airport? Except that it wasn't an act?'

'Something like that.' He smiled as he echoed her words.

'Mr Mackenzie? It *is* Mr Maximilian Mackenzie?'

Sally felt Max's arm stiffen behind her head, but he did not remove it. Oh, no, she thought, noting the camera slung from the newcomer's shoulder, surely not Mart Billing under another name?

'So what if I am?' was Max's familiar answer, as he clearly put his temper on a tight rein.

'It's come to the ears of the *Evening Rocket*——' the young man produced his card '—Stewart Mellidge—that you've got yourself another——' he cleared his throat '—I mean, a wife-to-be. Name of Sarah Dearlove? I might have got the surname wrong. Would this be the lady in question?'

There it was again, the query that revealed that yet another person couldn't quite believe that the celebrated Maximilian Mackenzie had dipped into the 'lucky barrel' of the female of the species and had been 'unlucky' enough to come up with her.

The lazy smile that Max turned on her told Sally he was saying, Over to you. It irked her that he now seemed to be enjoying himself.

'Who told you that tale?' she asked the reporter as sharply as if she were addressing a recalcitrant student in one of her classes.

A little abashed, the reporter answered, 'It's in all the gossip columns in the northern hemisphere. A—um——' he hesitated '—a contact over there passed the message on. And since you're in this part of the world, the place of Mr Mackenzie's birth, everyone'll want to know.'

A contact? It had to be Derek Winterton! Sally thought, aghast. She crossed her fingers tightly that Stewart Mellidge would keep his 'contact's' name—and her connection with him—to himself.

'And the rumour's just percolated Down Under?' she pressed, truly worried now. 'Don't you think it might have got just a little mangled and twisted by the distance that bit of gossip's had to travel?'

'If it's not true,' Stewart Mellidge said, plainly disconcerted, 'what are you doing here with his arm round you and you two looking as if you belong?'

'You think we look as if we belong?' was Max's amused question. 'Well,' with a slow raking glance of Sally's figure, 'maybe you're right. And maybe for once rumour's right too. Yes, "dear love"?' The smile in his eyes, let alone the curve of his mouth, threatened a complete meltdown of Sally's senses.

When he shifted position and that mouth made its determined way towards hers, she knew that her feelings for its owner wouldn't allow her to give it anything less than a delighted welcome. The very core of her seemed to be in the process of bursting into flames and she knew that not all the water gathered up from all the oceans of the world could—would ever—put out the fire.

'No, Max,' she heard herself whisper, 'it's not for real, you know that.'

It was as though she hadn't spoken. His head blotted out the figure of their interrogator, the passing footsteps and the whine of the lifts, the real world in its entirety. The sound of a voice raised in high-pitched laughter was the last thing Sally heard as that mouth, with its ever so slightly cruel curl, touched down on hers and took a kiss that robbed her not only of breath but of all protest and desire to resist.

When he lifted his head, his eyes kept on kissing hers, lingering on them and seeming to savour the taste of them all over again.

As a discreet cough penetrated the mist that floated magically around Sally's head, she felt an irritated movement of Max's shoulders and heard him clip the words, 'Flit, will you?'

Stewart Mellidge must have 'flitted'—his hastening footsteps told her that. Her secret link with Derek Winterton safe for the moment at least, Sally let out a secret sigh of relief.

Max did not shift, but continued to make remote-control love to her, his gaze straying from the cleft that the dive of her neckline allowed him to see, to the sweet swell of her breasts and down, over her hips and thighs, lifting finally to find her eyes again.

Even as he held them, his long-fingered hand moved to lift the gold locket that nestled in the softly perfumed valley of her burgeoning shape, his hard knuckles grazing the silky skin it found there. Her feminine responses leapt at his touch and she could not prevent her lips from trembling.

It seemed he could not resist their invitation, since his own seemed to tauten in anticipation and, with his knuckles still against her, the kiss he imparted this time not only robbed her of breath, but sent her pulses pounding in a mad stampede.

He lifted away from her at last, and Sally pushed at her hair, endeavouring to make sense of the bewildering confusion of her emotions. She couldn't—oh, heaven forbid—have fallen in *love* with him? No, she reasoned sagely, this feeling she had whenever he was near was her ego's flattered response to such a well-known man's attentions, arising though they did from his public image's temporary need of her.

Even so, when he gave her an amused and quite unreadable glance, then with a slow, deliberate movement replaced the locket between her breasts, letting his hand linger a moment longer than necessary, her heart took up the pace of an athlete's in training.

'You—you've missed your vocation,' she managed, trying to bring the situation back to normal. 'Your creative instincts should have led you in the direction of acting.'

'Acting-wise, Miss Dearlove,' he drawled, 'you're not doing so badly yourself. Unless,' his hooded eyes made her skin prickle, 'you respond as readily to any man's—er—sensual advances?'

She stiffened at the implied insult and made to leave him, angry warmth flooding into her cheeks, but his hand shot out, catching her wrist and pulling her back.

'Look at me,' he commanded, impelling her chin towards him against her stubborn resistance. His keen gaze read hers as closely as a doctor's examining an X-ray. 'You're trying to convince me, with your injured innocent act, that your social and sexual mores are the antithesis of those of your peers?'

Sally dislodged her chin from his hold. 'Let me take your points one by one, Mr Mackenzie.' It was the teacher in her surfacing, and by the faint curve of Max's lips she saw that he had recognised the fact. 'First, I am not *trying to convince* you. Second, my reaction to your provoking words wasn't an "act". Third, my morals are the personal and private rules I've devised as a result of observation, experience of living and what I want for myself, regardless of anything my friends and acquaintances of my own age group, i.e. *my peers*, may be doing. Do you understand?'

'Oh, I understand, Miss Dearlove,' he responded drily. 'The question is, does your boyfriend? Or,' with a cynical twist of the lips, 'do you have a different set of rules where he's concerned? I'm asking because I'm trying to place your very willing responses to me every time I act the lover.'

'That's the point, isn't it? You were *acting*, as I said. We both were, because that reporter was standing there.'

'And the other times?'

'At the airport? Likewise, because your fan Henni Curzon was there, waiting to be convinced, plus that other reporter, from the *Chronicle Weekly*.'

Anything, any explanation, she thought, to put him off the scent, to stop him from guessing how his kisses sent her heart into an uncontrollable spin. Only she would ever know how the fire he set alight reached out to him—and, she had to admit, to him alone.

'Anyway,' she added with a sideways glance, 'there was no need for you to go on kissing me after you heard him walk away.'

'Ah.' He smiled enigmatically. 'When you get to know me better, you'll also know that I hate unfinished business. I invariably like to bring to a conclusion, in this case, a very satisfactory conclusion, something I've begun,' he added mockingly. 'Come along, Miss Dearlove,' he stood, pulling her up by the hand, 'I'll see you to your room.'

In the lift, he said with a matter-of-factness Sally found it hard to adjust to, 'Tomorrow I shall probably be working for most of the day, so you'll be free to do as you please. I'll see you again at dinner.'

'Will you be writing?'

He inclined his head.

'Will there be lots of work for me?'

They had arrived outside her room. His own, it seemed, was next door. He took her key, used it and lifted her hand, placing the key on her palm and closing her fingers over it. Even a contact as light as that, she discovered to her dismay, set her pulses racing.

'Such eagerness to start her job!' he commented with a smile that set her nerves quivering. 'The answer to your question is, who knows? I might end the day surrounded by crushed pieces of paper.'

* * *

Sally awoke with a start to the ringing of her telephone. Certain that it was Max needing her services, she reached across eagerly to the bedside table and lifted the receiver.

'Your early morning call, Sally. Slept OK? I hope so, because I've got a serious proposition to make. Hey, are you awake, sleepyhead?'

Oh, no, Sally groaned, not the editor of the *Star and Journal* again!

'Mr Winterton,' she exclaimed agitatedly, 'you're wasting your money. The answer's no—I told you that yesterday. Please forget I ever wanted to join your paper.'

'And after I stayed at work extra late to call you all the way across the world! I'm going to double that amount I offered you for those stories I want about your fiancé. Also——'

'Correction, he's *not* my fiancé,' she interrupted. 'I'm his assistant——'

'Yeah? How come he said he thought himself lucky to have found such a wonderful dame to share his life with? I got that from Billing's follow-up piece about him. Mart's letting it out in tasty mouthfuls, leaving you wanting more. I intend to beat his Chronic *Chronicle* at its own game. I'm going to get it from the horse's mouth, if you'll forgive the expression, and that means you.'

'No,' she snapped.

'OK, how'd you like to become *Star and Journal*'s chief reporter?'

'With no experience? You're joking!'

'Joking I am not. With your educational qualifications, at least you'd know how to write good English, which is more than many so-called trained journalists do. I want those stories from you, Sally, and I'll tell you something else. Your uncle's backing me up. He also sends his congrats, by the way, on your engagement—to the great man, he means.'

Sally groaned, audibly this time.

'Ah, am I finally getting to you? Think, Sally. If it's a phoney engagement as you claim, it won't last, you realise? You'll come home needing a job. Give me what I want about your supposed fiancé and that job'll be waiting for you on this newspaper. Yes?'

No! she wanted to shout, but she closed her eyes, willing herself to think clearly, free of emotion, with reason and logic. It was true that she would need a job on her return. Back on home ground, Max would give her her marching orders as his assistant. After all, she was only standing in here for another person.

It was also true that, if she accepted the editor's proposition, she would be getting what she had longed for for years—a job as a journalist on a provincial newspaper.

'I——' she began.

'It's yes? Right.' Derek sounded jubilant. 'OK, ma'am. The contract's on its way. Have they got a fax machine in your hotel? They have? Right. Keep an eye open for a nice little document tied up with pink ribbon, addressed to you.'

'No!' she shrieked across twelve thousand miles. 'No contract, nothing in writing.'

A short silence, then, 'I get you. Nothing that the subject of our conversation might discover and ruin our little subterfuge. OK, let's call it a gentlemen's agreement between us—it'll be the first time anyone's called me a gentleman,' Derek joked, breaking the connection.

Breakfasted but scarcely refreshed—she suddenly had so much on her mind—Sally returned to her room and stared at the view. Longing to lift the receiver and dial Max's extension, she turned instead to the mirror, running a comb through her hair and making for the sunshine-flooded streets of the city.

Turning left, she walked beneath trees loud with the sound of cicadas, whose twittering song had so sur-

prised her on their long taxi ride from the airport to the
city centre. Passing the university, she glanced at the
buildings, seeing students standing in groups and feeling
the urge to join them and swap notes.

Retracing her steps, she walked down the hill, passing
the hotel and making for the downtown area. There were
shopping malls and enticing arcades, both modern and
also, Sally noted, restored to Edwardian splendour.

The lights changed and traffic from all directions came
to a halt, while pedestrians used all the crossings simul-
taneously. Then she found herself in Queen Elizabeth
Square, an attractive area near the waterfront, over-
looked by the Baroque-style main post office, which she
patronised, buying airmail letters with which to write to
her relations and friends.

Having coffee at a café in the shopping arcade near
the harbour, she wrote some cards she had bought from
a kiosk nearby. Then she took out the reporter's
notebook she had purchased along with the postcards
and, pencil poised, attempted to make some notes about
the man whose assistant she had agreed to become.

What troubled her so much was that she had also
tacitly agreed—by not turning down Derek Winterton's
latest offer—to write secret articles about the man she
now worked for. If she said—pencil to paper, she began
to make notes—how pleasant-natured he was, how strong
was his integrity, how devoted his fans were, even following him to the airport, surely Max wouldn't find
anything to object to in such statements, even if he were
to discover, which she was sure was unlikely, her secret
writings about him?

Entering her room, having lunched lightly in a pleasant
café in the town, she started to write in earnest, covering
two or three pages in no time at all. These she read
through, cutting and adding and finally dividing the
result into article-length pieces.

Gathering the sheets, she made her way down to the conference area and found the office in which she had discovered the fax machine. This she used, after some help from one of the hotel's secretaries, and sent her first editorial offerings on their way across the world.

Returning to her room, she started on another report, praising her employer to the skies. Yet, when her phone rang, having already guessed the caller's identity, she jumped so guiltily she bounced on the bed. Before answering the call, she pushed the notepad into a drawer.

'Sally? Where the hell have you been? This is the third time——'

'Wandering round the town. You gave me the day off, Max,' she reminded him edgily, guilt feelings renewed as her eyes came to rest on the drawer containing her clandestine notes. 'If you've got work for me——' A clatter filled her ear and she looked at the receiver as if it had tried to bite her.

More important, she wondered, what was biting Max? A few moments later she discovered the answer. And it wasn't work he held in his hand; it was a newspaper.

'*Evening Rocket.*' He threw the paper disgustedly on to the bed and strode to the window, hands thrust into pockets, bearing rigid, profile taut.

'Kiwi author Maximilian Mackenzie,' Sally read the confident headline, 'to marry British girl. Sarah Dearlove,' the ebullient report ran, 'ex-teacher turned author's secretary, mid-twenties and attractive and from the look of her as endearing as her name, is willing and eager to fill the gap that lovely Francine Anderley left in the life of Max Mackenzie, now aged thirty-five.

'Another side to Maximilian Mackenzie,' the report elaborated, 'is revealed in his new book *Grip of Night* which, his New Zealand publishers announce, he has come over to promote. Roald Beveridge, the main character, hates as passionately as he loves—and loses.

Is this the author himself, we wonder, still smarting at his so public rejection by his erstwhile lady-love, Francine Anderley? For picture,' the reporter directed, 'see page five.'

Sally gasped as she found the centre pages. There were the two of them in that passionate if meaningless clinch— well, it had been meaningless to Max—on the sofa they had occupied in an unobserved corner, or so they had thought, of the hotel's lounge-entrance foyer.

'How could they!' she exclaimed, horrified by the implications of the report, not to mention the compromising shot of them. Had she been so carried away by being in Max's arms that she had neither seen the flash nor heard the camera's click? 'You'll have to issue a denial, Max, at least of the first part.' He did not stir. 'Won't you?'

By the set of his shoulders and the slight tilt of his head, he seemed to Sally to have the air of a man torn by conflicting emotions, the sources of which, because she knew so little about him, were way beyond her understanding.

'How much,' he asked at last, 'does this boyfriend of yours mean to you?'

Good old plodding, honest Gerald, whom she didn't love and knew now that she never could? 'I'm—well, fond of him, I suppose. Why?'

'We're in this engagement thing deep, you and I.'

Her heart leapt at the thought of being in anything 'deep' with this man.

Softly she rose, approaching him, liking so much the way his hair brushed itself back from around his ears and changed direction around his lower hairline, turning inward. The resolute sweep of his jaw and the sharp outline of his nose gave his profile, to her who still went in awe of him despite having known his kisses and felt the strength of muscle in his enveloping arms, an intimidating dimension.

He must have heard her coming, but he did not react. 'Max,' she said softly, 'I'll go along with you, if it's what you want.' He turned his head at last, brows arched, facial expression telling her nothing. 'Carry on the pretence, I mean. It's been my fault from the start, hasn't it, that this "thing", as you call it, ever began?' His eyes sought the distant view again. 'I tripped and fell, threw my fruit juice over you.' She smiled, but he did not appear to see the joke. 'And weren't you angry, Max! Remember Henni Curzon, your devoted fan? It was she who linked us emotionally. It—it was a joke at first, wasn't it?'

'It's beyond a joke now,' he declared grimly.

'Or,' her heart began its familiar downward journey— deep down he really didn't want to know her, did he?— 'I'll get myself out of your life, then you can deny all that nonsense. Tell the whole story, if you like, at my expense. You're big, with your reputation and your success. Your integrity must be preserved at all costs. Say what you like about me. I'm small fry, I'll take it on the chin. Pack up the whole experience like a souvenir with my luggage, and when I get back home, I'll take it out and look at it and treasure it and...' She couldn't go on without giving herself away.

'And if I choose the first option?'

'Carrying on the pretence? I told you, I'm game. Oh, Max——' she stared unseeingly at the view he seemed to find so fascinating '—you'll never know how my life has changed since I shut the door on my rented flat and the closed-in life I'd known—it must surely be a lifetime ago—and threw myself at you.'

He lifted her chin and his smile grew so warm it caught at her very heartstrings, her lips quivering at the sympathy she felt reaching out from him. Only when he placed his on them did they grow still, then, in spite of her efforts to control them, part, the better to accept the pressure of his mouth.

This was no display of false passion put on for the benefit of an intrusive audience. This was human communication at its most compassionate. For long moments after the kiss ended, he was silent, looking at her, yet looking inward too.

At last he said, 'After the struggle it seems your life has been until now, after all you've given in the name of your parents' wellbeing, I don't know that I can ask you to act out this deception.'

Deception? If he but knew! Sally shook her head, but he persisted.

'It could mean a soul-destroying invasion of your privacy by outside forces, it could sometimes mean almost unbearable demands on your inner resources. More than that, it would mean your having to pretend to an emotional loyalty to me, not to mention an affection for me which you couldn't possibly feel, since you have a boyfriend of your own whom you profess to being fond of. Which I take to be a complete understatement of your true feelings for him.'

'Oh, but I——' You're wrong, she wanted to cry, he doesn't mean a thing to me. And I wouldn't have to pretend to love you, because I do, I do... With her face still tilted towards his, having just returned his kiss with so much warmth, if she had given voice to such sentiments he would believe them to have been spoken under the influence of her knowledge of his position in life, her inborn wish to help, as revealed in her past devotion to her parents in their time of need.

'I'm a good actress,' she managed at last, with a smile which, she hoped, would lighten the atmosphere and convince him that she was not taking the situation seriously. 'I'd enjoy it, honestly, Max. You—you don't know how, in recent years, I've longed for something exciting, something—well, glamorous, to happen to me.'

Had he swallowed her own little bit of deception? He released her chin and pocketed his hands.

'I've been your assistant, Max,' she said, her eyes smiling up at him, 'for—what, a couple of days? I'm game to add the job of being your temporary fiancée to my list of duties. With nothing in writing. So you could fire me on either count, or both if you liked, whenever you wished. Until we return home, or until there isn't any more need to pretend. Shall we shake on it?'

She put out her hand. He looked at it, he looked at her. Slowly his hand came out of its pocket and took hers in a grip so firm she gasped.

'Until there's no more need for pretence,' he confirmed. 'So, from this moment, Sarah Dearlove,' the way he said her name made her spine tingle, 'regard yourself as my wife-to-be.'

CHAPTER FIVE

THEY were to meet for dinner, Max had said. He had left her, in order, as he told her, to make yet another attempt to unblock the word jam.

Out of her wardrobe Sally slid a dress she had bought in a small boutique in downtown Auckland. Its lines were simple, its crinkle fabric clinging yet flowing, its translucence revealing more than concealing the attractive shape beneath. Clasping the chain of the gold locket around her neck, she fixed into place swinging gilt earrings with their imitation stones, a parting gift from Gerald, 'to remember him by', he had told her.

He probably wouldn't be happy to know that, since meeting the man for whom she now worked, she had hardly given him, Gerald, a thought.

It was strange, she reflected, but despite the falseness of her engagement to Maximilian Mackenzie she had begun to feel inside as if it were real, that she truly was his fiancée. Which was emotionally heady stuff, she acknowledged, and fraught with danger, not least because of her undercover involvement with the Press. And there was a reluctance deep down, a stubborn refusal, in fact, to take notice of the cautionary signals which her more down-to-earth self was emitting.

Turning from the mirror, she noticed an envelope which, she guessed, must have been pushed under her door as she had showered. Puzzled, she picked it up. It bore her typewritten name, and she wondered who might have known where she... Her spirits executed a dive from the heights to which they had unaccountably climbed. Derek Winterton! Oh, no, not now, not at this particular moment...

'Good work, pal,' the faxed sheet said. 'Carry on the way you've started and we'll make you assistant editor! Great so far, but we want more, *more* about the famous man you're currently affianced to. What about his moods, his temper, if he's got one—oh, boy, we hear he has—the colour of his shirts, how he makes love...?'

Sally ground her teeth and made to throw the paper from her, but checked her temper, feeling she should read the message to the bitter end. 'Come up with the goods, Sally Dearlove,' it went on, 'and we'll keep our promise to put you on the *Star and Journal*'s exclusive payroll. Derek W.'

How could she agree to write such intimate details about the man whose fiancée—she corrected her errant thoughts—mock-fiancée she had agreed to become? It would be betrayal of the most unacceptable kind. Yet, she reminded herself, when this pretence was over and she went back home, she would need a job, that job, the one she had wanted so much before she had left behind the safe, if care-burdened, life she had known.

A brief tap, then the door was opened. As Max turned to close it, Sally's hands moved convulsively to push Derek Winterton's missive into the drawer, adding it to the notes she had so hastily hidden away the last time Max had come to her room. Her guilty secrets were multiplying. Not long now, she thought despairingly, before they grew to the size of a mountain. Then what would she do?

Her cheeks burning, she sprang up and went to the mirror, running a comb through her hair. Her heart pounded as Max approached. He rested his hands on her half-bare shoulders and regarded her flushed reflection.

'Forgive the cliché, *dear love*, but has anyone told you how beautiful——?'

'Max, it's "let's pretend". You don't need to praise me.' His touch on her sensitive skin was unnerving her. She moistened her lips and regarded his mirror image. 'But I'll play ball. You look handsome too.' And, when the charade was all over and he had gone out of her life, not only handsome but threatening to the future tranquillity of her mind.

He laughed, massaging her shoulders, then releasing her. 'I expect you say that to your boyfriend every time you meet.'

'Oh, no, I—we——' Sally checked herself and managed a smile. 'Maybe I do.' Even so, a shrug of dismissal escaped her control.

They dined, Max ordering champagne, and they drank to each other as if the engagement was real.

'How do you like my acting, Max?' she queried, head on one side, towards the end of the meal. She'd had to ask the question if only to sober herself up, to bring herself back to reality. And to tell him silently that her flushed cheeks and overbright eyes were really all part of the role she was playing and were nothing to do with his potent effect on her.

'How do you like mine?' With a smile, he answered her question with his. 'Do I get the part in your play?'

'You can be my leading man any time you like,' she answered, laughing to imply that it was only a joke but secretly meaning it.

'Come with me.' They were standing in the entrance foyer, and Sally had been dreading the moment when Max would see her to her room and bid her goodnight. After all, in private, she reasoned, they need not carry on the pretence of being in love.

He took her hand and led her towards the arcade of shops within the hotel. In a spare moment, she had looked in their windows and lingered, but their high prices, even after being translated from dollars to her own currency, had sent her on her way.

Max halted her outside a jeweller's shop, its goods sparkling and shining in the brilliant lighting. 'Max?' she asked, frowning. 'Why——?'

He took her left hand. 'No fiancée of Maximilian Mackenzie would be without a ring on the appropriate finger.'

She jerked her hand from his. 'Oh, but I'm not——'

'Regard it,' he declared, unmoved, 'as a stage prop, or whatever you like. But,' his expression brooked no further refusal, nor even discussion, 'you *are* wearing my ring.'

She had no option but to follow him in. The assistant, on hearing his requirements, smilingly congratulated them on their engagement, then produced trays of rings whose stones and settings left Sally gasping.

'But, Max,' she murmured, hoping the assistant wouldn't overhear, 'these are far too good! There's really no need——'

'Try this.' As if she hadn't spoken, he had picked up an emerald and diamond ring on whose design her eyes had momentarily lingered. It fitted perfectly, and as she looked at it from all angles he asked, 'Or would you prefer a ruby or a sapphire?'

'No, no, this is beautiful, but please, Max,' she drew it from her finger and placed it on the velvet cloth on which the display was spread, 'it's far too costly.'

'Have you ever,' he asked the assistant, putting on a show of exasperation, 'met an engaged girl like this? One who tells her fiancé to put his money back in his pocket when he's about to buy her a ring?'

The girl behind the counter laughed, plainly thinking that Sally didn't know how lucky she was.

Max pocketed the small box, settling the account and taking Sally's hand as they left the shop.

'It's a beautiful ring,' she said, 'but——'

'If you dare to say "you shouldn't have", I'll throttle you!'

'All right, so I'll return it to you just as soon as our make-believe engagement is over.' She paused, waiting for his response. 'And if *you* had dared to say "You can keep it for services rendered", *I'd* have throttled *you*.'

He laughed. 'I wouldn't have dreamt of saying such a thing. It would have insulted your integrity, which I respect and admire, Miss Dearlove, more than I can say.'

Sally felt her heart jolt at such praise and once again a terrible sense of guilt flooded through her. How would he have described that 'integrity' with which he had endowed her had he known of her journalistic subterfuge?

But, she tried to defend herself, in those articles of hers that she had already submitted, she had not said anything bad about him, only good things. Surely that couldn't be regarded as a betrayal of confidences?

They walked for a while in amicable silence. Sally found herself wondering where Francine Anderley was nowadays, the woman he had, it seemed, loved and lost like the character in his latest bestseller.

It was dark by the time they reached the waterfront. Guiding her to a seat, beneath the harbour lights Max extracted the ring box from his jacket pocket and flipped it open, taking out the ring.

'Give me your hand. No, your *left* hand.' He pushed the ring into place, then tilted her chin, placing a kiss on her lips that held none of the compassion of his earlier kiss, and everything of a man whose entirely normal masculine reflexes had been activated by the very feminine characteristics of the woman at his side.

Any woman, not just me, Sally deliberately reminded herself in a desperate effort to clear her mind of the haze

in which she had unaccountably been drifting ever since
he had made his mock proposal.

His left arm drew her to him and her head found his
shoulder as if that was where it belonged and always
would. His hand rested just below her breast and she
fervently hoped that he couldn't feel the mad race of
her heart.

'The stars,' she whispered. 'Their constellations are
so different from the ones I'm used to.' Turning her head
a little, she pointed. 'There's the Southern Cross. Even
now I'm pinching myself to make sure that this isn't all
a dream and that I'm not really in the southern
hemisphere.'

'But you are.' His lips were warm and swift on her
forehead. 'Right here beside me on Auckland's
waterfront.'

She nodded against him, then her eyes roamed the
star-studded sky. 'The moon—I swear it's upside down.
I can't find the "man" in it that I've grown used to
seeing there since I was very young.'

'You're looking at it,' Max pointed out, 'from an entirely different angle.'

'Did you know,' she told him, 'that in my grandfather's memoirs he says how excited he was during his
five-year stay in Invercargill—he was a young man
then—to see Halley's Comet?'

'That was in, let me see, 1910?'

'Right. In New Zealand, he said, it could be seen with
the naked eye. He said it was a magnificent sight, with
its tail stretched right across the heavens.'

'You must show me his memoirs one day,' said Max.

Sally nodded and sighed with contentment, rubbing
her cheek against his shoulder. 'One day'. How wonderful that sounded, stretching into the future... He appeared to interpret her movements as those of tiredness,
as he rose and offered his outstretched hand.

Following her into her room, he watched, faintly smiling, as she gazed at the ring, holding it up to the light and admiring it. She was shaking her head, about to say 'You shouldn't have', when he silenced her protests by changing the subject, thus subtly reminding her of her true place in his scheme of things.

'I'm told by my publishers that my first promotional talk is scheduled for tomorrow evening. I'm reliably informed that my fan club will turn out in its dozens. Which probably means half a dozen,' he added with a dash of cynicism. 'You'll be free for that momentous occasion?'

Sally smiled at his sarcasm. 'How could I be otherwise? I can't wait to hear your talk.'

'I've got myself engaged, have I, to a devoted fan?'

'Sorry about it, Max.' She removed the ring and held it out. 'You can dis-enagage yourself right now if you——'

One stride and he was confronting her and the ring was back on her finger. 'Remove that at your peril!'

'Sorry,' she repeated. 'Of course, I'll need it for the meeting with your fans, won't I? It's not going to be that easy, Max, pretending to be your fiancée.'

'You really want to call the whole thing off?'

Vigorously she shook her head. That was the last thing she wanted! She would never see him again, would she, if this false engagement was ended here and now?

'The log jam—it partially unblocked itself today, which means I've got some work for you. OK?'

'Very OK,' Sally answered with a smile.

'I've arranged with the hotel's office section for the loan of a typewriter for your exclusive use. They've promised to bring you a desk and a typist's chair and anything else you might need.'

'That's fine. I——' she glanced at him doubtfully, 'I must warn you, Max, I'm not true secretarial material.

I was trained to use my critical faculties and judge other people's work objectively, and teach the children in my classes to do likewise.'

'Fine by me, Miss Dearlove,' he returned with a smile, 'just as long as you criticise my work constructively.'

'Criticise *your* work? I wouldn't dare!'

Laughing, he reached out and lifted the locket from between her breasts. 'This seems to be special,' he remarked.

'It is,' she answered when she had recovered from the sweet sensations caused by the touch of his hand in so sensitive a place. 'It was my father's last present to me before he died.' Then she thought of all the give-away information the locket contained and, remembering the weakness of its clasp, grew agitated as his hand continued to hold it.

'There's something I feel I must do, Max.' To her relief, he let the locket fall back against her. 'And that is, call my mother and tell her the truth about us.'

'Of course—go ahead. Have it on me.' She was shaking her head as he put up his hands and held it still. 'On me, and no arguments,' he said firmly. Tomorrow morning I'll bring that work. Goodnight, Sarah Dearlove.' His kiss was warm but swift, leaving her lips tingling for more.

He must have read the message in her eyes. He looked down at her, expression unreadable in the subtle lighting, then gathered her into his powerful arms. Lowering his head, he parted her lips, invading and savouring and depriving her completely of breath and all desire to resist, had it existed. Which it hadn't. His hand which, this time, had found its caressing way to her breast, lifted slowly.

'Sleep well, dear love,' came his husky whisper as he went on his way.

* * *

It was mid-morning time for her mother, Sally calculated, as she dialled the number. As she heard her mother's voice coming across those twelve thousand miles, a rush of homesickness and affection swamped her.

'Mum, I——' There was a catch in her voice.

'Oh, darling, I'm so pleased you've phoned! I didn't know where you were staying and I so wanted to tell you how delighted I was to hear the news. Look, Jeff and I will pay for this call. Just ring off and I'll——'

'Mum, there's no need. Max insists on paying.'

A little shriek from the other side of the world left Sally—the whole room—in no doubt of the extent of her mother's delight. 'How generous of your wonderful fiancé! If you'll forgive the old-fashioned expression, Sally, you've done so well for yourself. But then you deserve the very best, dear, because of all the sacrifices you made when your dear father was alive, and I—well, I——'

'Don't think about those times, Mum, they're over.' Tears welled as Sally faced having to tell her mother the truth. 'Mum, I must tell you something. It's not true that I'm engaged. It's all a mistake. Max and I, we——'

'Oh, Sally love, stop teasing! Oh dear, there's someone at the door. Write to us, Sally, write and tell us all about it. Goodbye, darling. And my love, too,' more shyly, 'to your wonderful husband-to-be.'

'My mother just wouldn't believe me,' Sally told Max worriedly next morning over breakfast. 'She wouldn't even let me explain.'

He was silent for some moments, stirring his coffee, saying at length, 'You've heard of the expression "willing suspension of disbelief", as when people read fiction or watch films or plays?' Sally nodded and found her eyes held by his. 'I suggest we do that, you and I, where this engagement of ours is concerned.'

'You mean,' she sought for the right words, 'that we submerge ourselves completely in the parts we're playing, and actually make *ourselves* believe it's real? Until the time comes to, as it were, break it off and go our separate ways?' Sally found that even saying those words was painful, but she hid her feelings with a smile.

Max smiled back. 'You must have been a good teacher, Miss Dearlove. Your definition is clear and accurate. The profession has suffered a great loss through your leaving it.'

Laughingly, she thanked him for his compliments. 'I had my reasons. All through my teens and even into my adult life, I wanted to be——' She brought her lips and tongue to a screeching stop. She had so nearly confessed to him her longing to be a journalist!

'To be a traveller, wandering the world?'

With immense relief, she nodded. His words had got her out of a very tight spot.

'So,' he continued, 'we've agreed, then, to convince the general public that our engagement is genuine——'

'*Your* public,' she amended, 'for the sake of your reputation as a writer——'

'—to immerse ourselves in our roles so well that, like the best actors, we're taken over by the characters we're playing and become them.'

'Agreed,' she whispered, acutely aware of all the questions that were straining at the bars of her mind in an effort to break free and be answered. What about in private? they were asking. What about the basics of all modern engagements, kissing and loving . . . and getting to know one another intimately?

'Shake on it.' Max's hand came out and, taking it, she searched his face. It told her nothing, like a blank page on which he had not inscribed a single word.

All day he worked, while Sally, in her room, used the hotel typewriter and did likewise, using room service for her meals. As she transferred Max's handwritten script into neatly typewritten paragraphs, she found the 'teacher' side of her admiring his phraseology, his gripping style, the way the words flowed and his characters sprang to life from out of the page.

All these things she could say about him, couldn't she, in an article for the *Star and Journal*? She found her own sheets of paper and, between working on the pages of Max's book, she typed her next article for Derek Winterton.

Hurriedly she corrected it, made a fresh copy and rushed down to the office to send its contents on their way through the hotel's fax machine. It didn't matter that the newspaper's staff might be at home and thinking of bed. There would probably be someone in the office working late, and in the receiving mode for offerings such as hers.

Racing back, she put her article aside and took up Max's work where she had left it, becoming absorbed once again in the words she was typing.

The room which the hotel manager had allocated to the Maximilian Mackenzie Fan Club overflowed with people. It possessed a raised platform with a table and a couple of chairs, which looked down on a few rows of red plush seating. Too few, it seemed, for the members of the fan club, many of whom were forced to stand wherever room could be found to place their feet.

Sally, to her acute embarrassment, had been invited by the excited lady secretary, who had introduced herself as Jean Browning, to join Max on the platform.

'Never let it be said,' remarked Mrs Browning with a dreamy smile, 'that the fans of the country of Mr

Mackenzie's birth had tried to part him from his beloved!'

Max, whose chair was only a foot or two from hers, leaned across and murmured with a satirical smile, 'Your first test, *beloved*,' Sally's heart leapt as, smiling, he emphasised the word Mrs Browning had used, 'in the role of my wife-to-be. All you have to do is to gaze up at me as if you adored me.'

I really do adore you, the words floated in and out of Sally's mind, but you must never know.

'They'll be so busy,' he went on under cover of the very high noise level, 'using their romantic imaginations and weaving their own stories around our supposed relationship, that they won't hear a word I'll have said about my own stories.'

'Not even,' she took him up with a nervous smile, 'if you suddenly lapsed into nonsense rhymes, or recited the alphabet?'

He laughed, and a wave of 'o-ohs' swept around the assembled company. They can see, Sally reflected, as I can, just how totally irresistible that action caused Max to look.

He had been right about his audience, she perceived. Although they plainly drank in every one of his words—some even using pocket recorders with which to tape his talk, and thus hear it at home all over again—the eyes of many, not excluding the men present, often drifted dreamily in Sally's direction, then back to their tall, distinguished guest. It was as if in their minds they were visualising them as bride and groom and delightedly hearing the words of the wedding ceremony.

'Did you notice,' Sally commented over coffee that evening as she and Max shared the same half-hidden lounge sofa as before, 'that the Press was present?'

'Mellidge of the *Evening Rocket*? I did.' There was a grating note to Max's voice that caused a shiver to course through her system. 'You know my opinion of his breed?'

Sally nodded. Only too well did she know! 'You used to be one yourself, or so your promotional blurb says.'

He inclined his head, but made no response.

'Thank you, Max,' she said, to divert the conversation into safer channels, 'for standing by me, literally, this evening. You let me follow you around like a—a——'

'Devoted pet?' Smilingly, he provided the words. His arm slid around her, his free hand taking hers. After all, she rationalised the action, some of his fans might still be around. 'Congratulations on your acting ability. How does this rate me for an Oscar award?'

Before she could even begin to feel embarrassed, his hand was around her throat, her arms sliding under his jacket, his mouth on hers. She found her own responding hungrily, her heart bounding kangaroo-like, her breath trapped in her lungs. This time she not only saw the flash but heard it too. An eager fan?

She felt the bones of his shoulders grow rigid and there was the faint graze of his teeth against her lips as his snarl began to form. He wrenched away, leaning forward menacingly. Stewart Mellidge stood there, wearing a sickly grin.

'Get out!' spat Max.

Sally leaned forward in line with Max. A glance showed her his unbounded fury and, afraid of what he might do, she gripped his arm. The camera went to work again, its flash blinding.

Max's feet hit the ground and he towered over their tormentor. 'Your equipment?' he clipped.

'No, the *Rocket*'s.' Stewart Mellidge held it to one side protectively.

Max's hand lifted and the camera crashed to the carpet, followed by Stewart's shriek of protest. 'A guy's gotta do his job, mate,' he moaned, crouching to pick up the pieces.

'Invade my privacy once more, *mate*,' snarled Max, his New Zealand accent coming through, 'and you—not to mention your editor—won't have a job to go to. Got it?'

Max's temper, Sally thought, trembling inside—'and has he got one!' she'd heard through the *Star and Journal*'s grapevine. And hadn't he just! she thought fearfully.

Nursing his damaged equipment, Stewart Mellidge walked away.

'Max, should you——?' Sally began.

His cold glance stopped her. 'Yes?' Those lips that had so recently lifted from hers were taut and forbidding. If he hated journalists that much, she thought, what would his reaction be to her if he ever discovered her links with 'that breed', as he called them? But he mustn't, she told herself fiercely, not ever.

Entering her room, Sally walked to the window. Max followed her in, closing the door. She wished she knew how to cope with his mood, a spin-off still, she guessed, from their fiery encounter with the Press.

He strolled across to join her, turning her to him. So relieved was she at his change of demeanour, she went eagerly into his arms, willingly giving up her lips to his. She found herself clinging, a longing truly to belong to him, to do his bidding without constraint, rising within her like a river in flood.

As his hand slid beneath her low-cut top and cupped her throbbing breast, her lips parted on a gasp and he fitted his mouth over hers in a kiss that was both persuasive and demanding.

'Sally Dearlove, Sally... *dear love*,' she heard him whisper. 'Do you know what you do to me?'

'It's just—just that you're a man,' she whispered back in reluctant explanation, 'and I'm a woman, so isn't it natural, even though our engagement isn't real?'

'Can I help it,' he queried with a crooked smile, 'if the character I'm playing is taking me over?'

'It's taking me over too, Max,' she answered huskily. 'You're doing strange things to me.' She ran her finger over his mouth, trying to push the corners into an upward curve, although as merely his mock fiancée she told her finger it really had no right.

If he would only smile, she thought, it would break the spell. Pointedly she looked around the room. 'No one watching, Max, so there's no need to play-act, is there?' She was desperate for him to drop the pretence. Much more and she knew she would be unable to refuse whatever he might ask of her.

He seemed to sense her tension and let her go. Her eyes followed him to her desk, watching him pick up the bulging folder into which she had pushed his script.

'Sorry the pages aren't in order,' she said. 'I was in such a hurry to get ready for dinner, I left them until later.'

'That's OK.' He went to the door. 'I have a rule never to look back until a book is finished. I rarely break it. Goodnight, Sally.' His smile lingered in her eyes even when she closed them to sleep.

CHAPTER SIX

SALLY lifted the phone. 'Hi, Max,' she greeted him with a smile in her voice, 'any work for me this morning?'

She had spent most of the night dreaming about him. He had smiled at her all through the dark hours, lighting them up like a hundred suns, and she still hugged their warmth and brightness to her heart.

'Some,' he told her.

Sally waited for him to continue, but the silence lengthened so much she wondered if he was still there. He had not appeared for breakfast. She assumed he had used room service, although he had not told her of his intention, as he had promised he would.

'Will you be bringing——' No, he was Maximilian Mackenzie this morning, that much, she told herself, was plain. 'Shall I come and get the work?'

'Why not?'

His moods, she reflected as she tapped on his door and went in, were something she would no doubt learn to understand and cope with as time went by. Except that the man who stood there, hands in pockets, dark cotton sweater over open-necked shirt, casual trousers that hugged his hips, was someone she had seen only once before, and that was last night when he had dealt so ruthlessly with a representative of the Press.

'B-bad dreams?' she queried, smiling bravely in the face of his unbending stance.

'Very.'

'Still angry about Stewart Mellidge? I don't blame you. You were right about him invading your pr——'

85

'The work's over there. Tomorrow we move on. I've hired a car. We go south to Rotorua. I have an evening lecture there, followed by a social gathering. Be packed by tonight, will you? I'd like an early start.' He turned away. It was a dismissal, no doubt about it.

This was the celebrated novelist with a vengeance, Sally thought, her heart trailing behind her as she returned to her room, the great man putting his assistant-cum-secretary right back in her place. What was a kiss—or two or three—between acquaintances, anyway?

Half an hour later the phone rang.

'I'm going for a walk,' Max told her. 'If there's any query, it'll have to wait until I'm back.'

'Yes, Max,' she began, all obliging secretary, which it seemed was how, for today at least, he wanted her to behave, 'but your writing's so clear I doubt if I'll——' There was a crash in her ear and she found herself addressing the receiver.

Hand to her head, she wandered round the room, sitting down, starting to work, getting up. Something was biting him, she was certain of that. Sighing and shaking her head, she tackled the fresh pages of script.

Halfway through the morning, as she sat, hands poised over the typewriter keys after a short break, a frighteningly possible explanation of Max's strange behaviour erupted in her mind. The words she was in the process of typing jumbled themselves up before her very eyes, dancing about and forming themselves into nonsense.

Oh, God, no! she thought, hand to her throat. That article she had written and sent off by fax machine to the *Star and Journal*—when she had brought it back from the hotel office she had dropped it on to her desk along with Max's script! Or had she after all put it into her drawer? Not a sign of it there. A tremble took hold and she felt hot with embarrassment and shame and self-reproach. How could she have been so careless?

She walked about the room, recalling her haste in shuffling together the pages which had been strewn all over her desk, then rushing for a shower. Later, she had promised herself, she would put them in order—except that last night Max had taken the folder, *and she had been so bowled over by his kisses she had forgotten all about her own small effort mixed in with his...*

'I never look back at my work until the book's finished,' he'd said. Hope rose like the sun on an icy expanse. Maybe his mood this morning had really been a hangover from his furious encounter with the *Rocket*'s reporter?

He had gone for a walk, hadn't he? Wrenching her door open, she sped to the lift and made for reception.

'May I——' she moistened her lips, smiling at the receptionist and crossing her fingers behind her '—may I be permitted to borrow the key to my—my fiancé's room? He's gone out and there's something I need to find in connection with his work.'

Recognising Sally and knowing of her supposed relationship to Max, the girl handed over the precious key without hesitation.

The folder was on his writing table, and with shaking hands, Sally sorted through the disorder of pages. The vital typed sheet was missing. Which could only mean...

'Panning for gold, Miss Dearlove?'

The icy tones had her spinning round, her breaths coming fast, her heart taking hurdles. Conscience-stricken, she could only stare at him.

'I was—I'm sorry,' she managed, 'but...I th-thought you were out.'

'That's bloody obvious.' His lips were a straight line, his eyes flashing cold fire. 'I came back—too soon, it seems, for your purposes. Is this,' three strides took him to a low table, 'what you're looking for?'

Sally just prevented herself from snatching the paper. He'd seen it now, she told herself miserably, so what was the use? 'Thank you, yes.' She took it and stood in front of him with as much dignity as she could muster. Might as well hold her head high, she resolved, when the axe fell.

'What was the motivation?' he asked tonelessly.

'For wr-writing about you? Well,' she searched her article for clues as to how to answer, reassuring herself that she had made no mention of Derek Winterton, nor even typed in the *Star and Journal*'s name. As it stood, it gave no sign of its destination. 'Maybe,' she threw in, hoping to distract him, although hating herself for doing so, 'as a—a teacher of English——' She turned to the door. 'I'll—I'll——' Anything to get away from his stony expression, the unbearable suspicion in his eyes.

'I—er—assume those were notes for one of your classes? When you return to base and to teaching?'

Oh yes, she thought, what a way out, what an escape from her predicament!

She managed to smile self-deprecatingly. 'Once a teacher, always a—I mean, I was trying my hand at a——'

'Profile of a writer?'

'Maybe I was.' Why was he feeding her with excuses, giving her ways out of the mortifying situation in which she found herself?

The silence was so long she found her hands folding the typewritten sheet, then folding it again. She looked at him, looked away. 'I—I'm sorry, Max,' she whispered. 'I'll pack my things——'

'Just as long,' a couple of strides brought him nearer, his expression softening the merest fraction, 'just as long, Miss Dearlove, as the breed I love to hate doesn't get its grubby hands on your scholastic offerings.' His hand came out, in demand, not in greeting, but not, to her relief, for her article. 'It's as well, isn't it, that reception had a spare key for this room?' This she gave him.

There was a noticeable drop in temperature between them for the rest of the day. Even over dinner, Sally felt as well as saw the coolness in Max's eyes. They talked in a desultory way, with long silences in between. Now and then Sally found his eyes on her, but she couldn't meet them. Eating at her was the growing possibility of his somehow discovering her secret. She hadn't stopped all day reproaching herself for her carelessness.

The frightening thing was that, given their present way of life—moving on, working, then moving on some more—there was no certain way of making sure that such an error didn't happen again.

Yes, there was! she thought later, alone in her room as bedtime approached. I'll fax Derek Winterton a letter that will put a stop to the entire arrangement.

Hurrying to her desk, she wrote: 'From this moment on, please note that there will be no more articles from me about Maximilian Mackenzie. He trusts me too much for me to fail that trust by acting as a kind of journalistic spy on his character, his moods, his sexual prowess—you never would have got that out of me anyway—and the way he works to produce his best-sellers.'

'All I can say,' her letter continued, 'is that he's a wonderful man, honest and straightforward and considerate—all characteristics I admire, which is why you won't be hearing from me again on the above-mentioned subject matter.'

'Finally,' she added, 'although our "engagement" is false, we are, for many reasons, both personal and practical, treating it as though it's real, which means I must be loyal to him at all costs. Anyway, Mr Winterton—and this is a secret I'm entrusting with you—*don't you ever tell anyone or I'll sue*—I love him so very much I would never, ever, do anything to hurt him. I'm withdrawing from the Mackenzie assignment. If it means I'll never get into journalism, then so be it. This is final. We're moving on. Please don't try and contact me again. Love to my uncle—that is, what I can spare from loving Max. Sarah Dearlove.'

Lying on her bed before dinner in the new hotel room and listening with growing wonder to the sounds of the incredible landscape outside, Sally recalled the day she had spent at Max's side as he had driven south to their destination.

On the way, they had visited the famous Waitomo Caves, wandering through massive limestone chambers and forests of great white and many-hued stalagmites and stalactites. They had looked upon unbelievable rock formations with names like Organ Loft and Banquet Chamber and Cathedral and peered down dark and awe-inspiring holes.

On an underground river, they had floated in a boat through the Glow-worm Grotto. In the darkness, they had seen the fantastic sight of millions of glow-worms shining like stars above their heads. The boatman had called for absolute silence, with not even a whisper to disturb the glow-worms, guiding the boat by means of his hands against the rock walls, or using hand-over-hand movements on overhead lines.

Max's arm had come round her as she had tilted back her head, her eyes as starry as the massed pinpoints of light above them.

'Oh, Max,' she had exclaimed as they had emerged, blinking hard, into the daylight, 'it's an experience I shall never forget!'

'I've seen it before,' he had told her, 'but I particularly wanted you to see it.'

'It's something,' she had said, finding his words curiously pleasing, 'that the whole world should see.'

In the boat in the semi-darkness, her mind distracted by the fantastic scene around them, she was unaware of how the rest of her had snuggled up to him—until she felt the pressure of his lips on her hair.

Her eyes had sought his in the light of the glow-worm 'stars', and with a sweeping sense of relief she had found in them a return of the warmth they had once held and whose absence she had felt so acutely in the past two days.

Had he believed the explanation he had unknowingly helped her to invent? Had he, she wondered, forgiven her? Had his trust in her returned?

After the lecture, the social gathering, as Max had called it, went with a swing. The fan club appeared to have discovered in advance that Max's and Sally's engagement had come out into the open on New Zealand soil, the country of his birth. In celebration of the fact, it had unanimously and delightedly decided to buy some bottles of champagne with which to toast the couple's happiness.

Afterwards, the fans crowded round with copies of Max's latest book, clamouring for his signature. For a while Sally, mindful of her role, not just as his 'fiancée', but as his assistant, watched at his side, as pleased as if she had really been his wife-to-be to hear the fans' outpourings of praise and to see their obvious admiration for their homespun yet world-acclaimed literary hero.

Slipping away unobserved by the happy throng, Sally wandered around, leaving Max to it.

During the lecture she had noticed at the back of the large room a young man seated alone. He was there still, speaking to no one, drinking his champagne and popping the odd savoury into his mouth. He was more casually dressed than the women fans, and Sally deduced that he was something of a loner. He must be too shy to socialise, she reasoned, and, donning a friendly smile, she made her way towards him.

Seeing her approach must have frightened him further into his shell of shyness, since he made frantic efforts to tuck away his notebook—a number of the fans had taken a careful record of every word Max had uttered—and slip from the scene.

'Mr—er—' Sally called to him, 'if you'd like Mr Mackenzie to sign your book, he'd be only too pleased.' But he had hit the swing door and made it to the street before she could reach him.

Tiredness caught up with her, but it was clear that the devoted fans had by no means finished with their hero. Managing through sheer determination to break into the mini rugby scrum, Sally reached Max's side. Deep in conversation though he was, she touched his hand.

To her astonishment, he jumped as though she had stung him. He stood at once, swinging towards her.

'It's been a long day, darling,' she murmured softly. The endearment felt strange on her lips, but she was certain it was the one word that his devotees had been waiting for, 'so if you don't mind, I'll go up and get some sleep.'

An eyebrow quirked, but only for a second. To her relief, he was quick to catch on. Before she knew what was happening, she was in his arms and on the receiving end of a devastating kiss.

It was as though, besides signing dozens of books, he had also scrawled his signature across every woman's romantic heart. They sighed with pure contentment, as if their own private dreams had come true.

In the fading daylight, Sally stepped through the sliding windows on to the balcony and looked out over the unbelievable panorama which spread itself far and wide beneath her. Below her room there was a bubbling cauldron, a boiling mud pool that formed strange curved shapes on its thick, ever-moving surface, with circles whose rings spread out to the rim like pleated ripples.

The strong sulphur smell which had assailed her nostrils from the moment of their arrival in the town—'like a chemistry lab', Max had referred to it—strangely did not seem quite so potent. Her sense of smell, she assumed, must have adjusted to it, accepting it.

Wherever she looked, steam was rising from the land, while, fascinatingly, in the middle distance, from the midst of shrubs and trees fountained a spectacular column of steam from a geyser. It roared and feathered over the air and lifted high in the breeze, greeting with a twisting, turning kind of anger the moon's rising appearance.

'You're honoured,' said Max's voice behind her as he advanced to stand at her side, 'Pohutu doesn't often put on such a exhibition of power and beauty for the tourists.' A short pause, then with an edge, 'Who was the male I watched you pursue after the lecture?'

Sally smiled. 'A very shy fan of yours, as far as I could judge. I called out to him that you'd be pleased to sign his book, but he made his getaway as if a horde of elephants was after him.'

'Into public relations, are you, in a big way?' The words might have had a sarcastic ring, but the tone that delivered them had softened.

He turned her by the shoulders, his hands sliding down to follow the slender shape of her, lingering on her hips while his thumbs moved inwards to rotate over sensitive hollows.

'The guide book says,' she managed hoarsely, as slowly and subtly the movements brought a mounting warmth to her loins, 'that Pohutu's the most famous of all New Zealand geysers.'

Max nodded, eyes preoccupied as he spanned her waist, fingertips not quite meeting. The wrapover top gaped under the pressure and the smooth whiteness of the upper slopes of her breasts peeped out shyly in the light of the rising moon.

The locket she habitually wore rested in their valley and he lifted it out of the way, placing his lips where it had nestled. Hardening his hold, he contained the shiver his kiss had forced out of her.

'Pohutu is moody and no one knows for certain just when it will blow.' He had spoken absently while his hold moved ever higher, cupping her breasts. Then, growing impatient with the small amount of flimsy fabric that kept his palms from immediate contact, he slid the dress from her shoulders.

Now her breasts spilled out and glowed in the semi-darkness and she threw back her head, gasping, as his head lowered and his mouth teased and nipped and aroused in her a throbbing need that dried her mouth and caught her breath in her lungs.

'Lift your arms,' he growled, 'put them around me. By heaven,' his glittering eyes netted hers, 'are you as inhibited as this with your boyfriend?'

'Max, we—I——' she whispered, her voice so small she could hardly hear her own words, 'I don't——'

'Respond when he makes love to you? No wonder he let you come away alone!' He pulled her hard against him and she felt his unmistakable arousal beneath the casual clothes he had changed into after the shower she knew he had taken because of the dampness of his hair as it had brushed her skin. Through teeth that seemed puzzlingly to be gritted, he said, 'Do I have to teach you the ways of a woman who lies——' he checked himself, then went on, '—lies with a man who's her fiancé?'

'But, Max,' she responded hoarsely, 'you never said that you wanted this from me. Remember we're not really——'

'Oh, it's real enough, Miss Dearlove, this link between us,' he returned on a strangely cynical note. 'You have my ring. I've offered you my name. On a purely temporary basis, of course, a condition you accepted. An engagement lasting a few months, maybe even a year, which, as relationships go in these *emotionally enlightened* days,' the emphasis was cuttingly sarcastic, 'is as reasonable a length of time as anyone might expect. So let yourself go, Sarah Dearlove, suspend your disbelief, as I have. I'm deeply into this role of husband-to-be to you, and in the best literary tradition I'm letting the part I'm playing of your lover take over my own character and lead me to its ultimate goal—your bed.'

It was like a hurricane, this feeling he was creating inside her, lifting her off her feet and rendering her unable to help herself. It was like a tidal wave crashing down and drowning her, depriving her of all power, and will, to resist.

'You've bewitched me, witch,' Max said huskily, on a softer note, 'with your eyes full of challenge, yet bedevilled with uncertainty. Your worldly wisdom mixed with a refreshing, almost childlike approach to everything around you. Whatever there is to come where our relationship's concerned, however much in the future our paths might diverge, I want you, lady, and I want you *now.*'

He impelled her backwards to stand beside the bed, then held her upright, jaw thrust forward, eyes diamond-hard.

'If you ever two-time me, Sarah,' he said in a voice that sent spasms of dread raging through her, 'if I ever discover you've betrayed my trust, I swear I'll——' His fingers fastened around her throat.

'Th-throttle me?' she finished, croaking with a terrible foreboding.

'You've said it, baby,' he answered, 'oh yes, you've said it.'

Slowly he bent her beneath him, his mouth against hers, parting her trembling lips and thrusting deeply into its moist and tender cavities, letting her fall at last on to the bed's yielding softness.

He came down on top of her, crushing her, making her gasp for breath. Her arms coiled themselves round his neck and her breasts hardened against the mat of hair on his chest which had somehow become bared as he had descended.

A choking cry was torn from her as something cut into the flesh between her breasts and Max jerked away, lifting himself from her.

Reaching out, he switched on the bedlight. With astonishment mixed with horror he stared down at the small incision oozing blood which had even managed to smear itself over his own chest.

'My God, what——?'

'My locket,' Sally gasped, feeling for it as he broke away. 'The catch is faulty. It's always coming open. The inside edges dug into me.' She sat up shakily. 'My—my boyf——' In the circumstances, it was embarrassing beyond words and completely out of place to use such a word. 'Gerald mended it, but it's obviously still faulty. Max,' seeing the bloodstain on his skin, 'I'm terribly sorry. I'll get something to——'

'Forget about me. It's you who needs mopping up.' He removed the locket, dropping it to the bed, and, reaching for a tissue, gently staunched the wound.

At last the bleeding stopped and, her cheeks warm at the intimacy of the situation—she had not yet had a chance to lift her dress into place—Sally found a plaster which Max insisted on applying.

Fastening her dress, she thanked him and looked around for the locket. To her dismay, its contents had spilled on the floor and, dreading the inevitable questions, she watched Max retrieve them one by one.

'Who's the man?'

'I told you,' silently Sally cursed her well-intentioned ex-colleague, who had slipped out of his place in the locket. 'Gerald mended the clasp, or thought he had, and put his photograph in it before giving it back to me.'

'And you left it there?' His tone was so frigid it was as though the window had swung wide open, letting in the cool night air.

With a shrug which she hoped would minimise her apparent oversight, she answered truthfully, 'I just didn't bother to remove it.'

'So you brought his image with you after all? And yet you let me make love to you, almost allowing me to go the whole way?'

How could she tell him, 'I couldn't resist you'? That any feeling she might ever have had for Gerald had paled into insignificance against the almost uncontrollable sensations Max aroused in her, against the *love* she felt for him?

'I—I've known Gerald for some years. He's a friend. He'd like to be more, but——'

'You can't make up your mind?'

'Put it that way if you like.' Wearily she rose from the bed. The rest of the locket's contents, alarmingly revealing, lay exposed.

'My mother's address,' she explained quickly, 'in case of accid——'

'I thought,' Max cut in, seemingly puzzled, 'that you said his name was Gerald?'

'It is. Why?' Then she remembered and tried to snatch back the scrap of paper.

'Derek W.,' Max read out. 'Another male *friend* to add to the list?'

Oh, heavens, Sally bemoaned silently, was this the end? Was her awful secret about to be forced into the open? Then she remembered that she had only made a note of Derek Winterton's extension at the *Star and Journal*. That newspaper's London number she knew by heart.

'Maybe,' she answered with a tremulous smile, her heart thumping so loudly she was sure he could hear. 'If I have got a list, doesn't that prove that no one is special to me?' Except you, she longed to add.

The telephone's ring tore into the taut silence. Max, being nearest, lifted it. 'Sarah Dearlove's room.'

'Is Sally there?' Loud and clear, the voice came over the thousands of miles and Sally nearly fainted. 'Tell her, will you, that this is D—...oh, my God!'

Sally, panicking, wrenched the receiver from Max. 'How did you know where I was?' she demanded.

'Contacts at your end—*Evening Rocket*. For Pete's sake, if you know what's good for you, get off the line pronto.' The crash from the other end almost damaged her eardrums.

She tried a smile, but it was so shaky she wished she hadn't. 'He m-must have fainted,' she explained.

'Gerald? At finding another man in your room?' Max asked with a sardonic smile. 'Or was it Derek?'

'It m-might have been Derek,' she agreed weakly.

It certainly had been Derek who, on realising just who had answered Sally's phone, had plainly decided to sink to the bottom of whichever ocean between the two calls was the deepest.

At the door, Max paused. 'Where,' he said with a sarcastic smile, 'will you put me on your lovers' list? Tacked on at the end?'

'At the very top, Max,' she answered truthfully, tossing back her tousled hair and feeling the moisture gather on her brow at her fantastically lucky escape.

CHAPTER SEVEN

THREE days later Max told her, 'I'm throwing my schedule overboard.'

They had spent the time working, interspersed with sightseeing. He had driven her around the area, letting her see rocks and cliffs with mists of steam rising out of them and boiling waterfalls, while steam rose even out of hot streams and ponds.

'You've done me proud, Max,' Sally told him after an exciting few hours wandering around a thermal wonderland not far away.

Max had shown her cold pools and hot, hissing and steaming, of every hue—yellow and orange and green and black—some even changing colour as they watched. Her hand holding fast to Max's, Sally had gasped at boiling shallow craters the colour of ink, one being called the Inferno Crater, whose depths were filled with violently boiling mud.

There was a pool called Champagne because it bubbled like its namesake, and another, called Artist's Palette, whose shades of every hue changed constantly.

'Max,' she had gazed up at him, 'I'm so enjoying my stay in your country. I love it so much.' Not least, she thought, because you're with me.

'You,' he murmured, pulling her to him and kissing her, 'to coin a phrase, "ain't seen nothin' yet." There's so much more waiting out there. The South Island, for instance, with its green fields reaching into the far distance, wall-to-wall with sheep. Not to mention the Southern Alps, and mountain ranges capped with snow, plus glaciers and icefields and rain forests and mangrove swamps. However,' he let her go, withdrawing a little into himself, 'you're not likely to see it for a while. I've rung the Auckland office and cancelled the next couple of lectures and book signings.'

'So where are we going instead?' Where, she wondered, did she fit into his altered schedule, if at all?

'To visit my relatives.'

He was taking her to meet his family? 'Your parents?' she queried.

'No. My aunt and uncle, my grandfather, and anyone else who happens to be around. My mother lives back in the old country, where I've made my home. My father died when I was a boy.'

'I'm sorry about that.' How little she knew of him, of his life before they met. But there had been no need to know, had there, before that foolish accident of hers had tipped her—and tripped her—headlong into his life?

'Do I——?' She moistened her lips. 'Do I wait in the car, Max, while you're seeing them?'

He laughed. 'For a couple of days?'

'Is that how long you're——'

'We. Two, or maybe three. It depends.'

'But,' didn't he understand how difficult it would be for her? 'do they know the true situation between us?'

There was a long pause and the green countryside passed tranquilly by.

'Tell me, Sally, what is the true situation between us?'

She looked at him sharply, a tiny stab of fear catching her under the ribs. What did he mean?

'You know, Max. That we're only pretending.'

Fields rose into rounded hills, farmhouses tried to hide themselves in the dips and hollows.

'Would you be able to keep up that pretence,' he asked at last, 'under the close scrutiny of my fond relatives?'

'It would mean pretending, wouldn't it, that I loved you, that we—loved each other? Could *you*,' she turned the tables with an over-bright smile, 'keep up the pretence? Well enough to be convincing, I mean, while you're among people who know you much better than I do?'

His gaze flicked her face, his lips curving in an enigmatic smile. But his answer was brutally frank, shocking her.

'It isn't difficult for a normal, red-blooded male to pretend to love an attractive woman. Which, although you may not know it, you undoubtedly are.'

'Nor,' she hit back to assuage the hurt his words had inflicted, 'is it difficult for a woman to *pretend* to love a husky heart-throb of a celebrated author, whose books are read the world over and whose success has brought him an overflowing bank account.'

'Wow,' came the soft answer, 'can this lady teacher draw blood when she's aroused! Tell me, Miss Dearlove, did any of your students go home limping sometimes from some of your sarcastic comments?'

Sally turned away tight-lipped, her ego still smarting under the lash of his plain speaking. But wasn't she the fool, she castigated herself, to believe that his kisses and caresses had meant anything? Except that as a man he had been aroused by her proximity—not to mention her undisguised willingness to allow him to attempt to seduce her?

'I think the score's even, Sarah,' he remarked, turning at last on to a stony road which curved its way between fields packed with sheep. 'After due discussion, we find ourselves in agreement about continuing to pretend our false engagement is real until, as we've already decided, the time comes for it to be broken off. Yes?'

'Yes,' Sally answered, a strange sense of relief sweeping over her. He was hers for a little longer, hers to look at with open admiration, to receive his kisses, to hold his hand and feel his arms come round her whenever his reading public demanded a display of affection.

The house was called Totara Lodge, named, Max explained, after a native New Zealand tree. It was built of wood, in common with the majority of the country's houses, its dormer windows pushing free of a corrugated iron roof.

Even if the welcome had not been warm, which it was, Sally would have taken pleasure from the feeling of serenity she experienced the moment they entered. The colour scheme was a cool green, offset by the soft peach of the curtains and carpets.

'Max, my dear,' his aunt's arms reached up and hugged him, 'how good to see you! Your uncle Ron will be so disappointed at missing you—he's in Christchurch on business. How long is it since you were in this part of the world?' she asked, releasing him.

'Two years or more,' a gruff voice behind her supplied.

'Grandfather!' Max smiled with obvious affection. 'Great to see you looking so well.'

'You should come more often,' the tall, white-haired man commented. Handshakes and yet more hugs were exchanged. 'You've got the spare cash, from what we hear, so no excuse. We see your books on sale all over, and we're so proud, lad. But just look who he's brought us!'

Sally, who had been hovering shyly behind Max's broad back, stepped to his side and was herself the recipient of an 'aunt' hug, followed by a warm kiss on the cheek.

'It's good to meet you, Mrs Hayward,' Sally said, finding her hand passed along the line and her cheek being warmly kissed by Max's grandfather.

'Call me Grandfather, dear,' he invited. 'Everyone else does.'

'Yes, Grandfather,' Sally responded, and with a falsely reproachful glance over her shoulder at Max she added with a smile, 'I can't say I've heard a lot about Max's family, because I haven't.'

'And call me Aunt Delia, dear,' Mrs Hayward told her, 'it won't sound so formal. After all, you're going to be one of the family, aren't you? We've heard so much about you,' Aunt Delia declared. 'Max has called us almost every day since he arrived in the country, haven't you, Max? It's been Sally this and Sally that.'

'It hasn't!' protested Sally.

'Yes, dear, it has. You see how fond of you he is. I'll tell you a secret.' She pretended to whisper. 'He's particularly fond of saying your surname.'

Sally laughed, turning bright eyes to Max. 'You're right about that. I don't know why.'

At which they all laughed.

Sally was astonished to hear of Max's numerous phone calls. Which could only mean that he had known from the start of their tour where he was heading for. Yet he hadn't told her.

But why should he? she argued. All along, she had really been Max's employee, not his fiancée. And as for his mentioning her name so frequently in his calls to his aunt, he was no doubt rather cleverly paving the way for her entrance, and acceptance, into his family.

'He really has fallen hard this time, haven't you, Max?' smiled his aunt.

He smiled an enigmatic smile and declined to answer.

Fallen hard? Max's acting, Sally decided, must surely merit an Oscar. And 'this time'? She tried not to let that hurt.

'Oh, what a lovely ring, Sally! Look, Grandfather. It's even better, Max, than the one you——' Aunt Delia's smile did not falter as adroitly she changed the subject. 'Now, dears, how about a nice cup of tea?'

The March afternoon glowed warmly around them. They drank their tea seated on chairs on a raised wooden platform beneath a canopy held in place by white-painted poles. Down the steps was a swimming pool, blue as the sky, which was cloudless in the late summer sun. The garden, flower-filled and lovingly attended, reminded Sally of her home country.

They talked and laughed, drank a limitless supply of tea and consumed homemade fruit-bread and cakes, warm from the oven. Neighbours and friends drifted in and out, having been invited especially to meet the famous nephew, his manner, like his clothes, relaxed and informal. To Sally's astonished eyes, he even seemed happy.

Everyone shook Sally's hand and welcomed her warmly to their country, saying how delighted they were that their neighbours' nephew and grandson respectively had found such a lovely wife-to-be.

As the evening progressed, Sally produced her grandfather's memoirs, and with Max's grandfather beside her, they pored over the postcards and newspaper cuttings which had been inserted into the manuscript which her grandfather had bound in a folder and indexed with loving care.

Max hovered in front of them, rebuking Sally lightheartedly, his eyes warm and approving, 'You show them to my grandfather, but not to me, although I've asked to see them.'

'Join us, Max,' invited his grandfather, taking him seriously. 'There's a cosy space all ready for you beside your dear lady.'

Sally glanced up quickly, catching Max's mocking smile. His 'dear lady'? How she wished she were!

'My dear love, don't you mean?' Max queried,

He was using her name again, she noticed, hugging to her heart the way he said it, as though he really meant it. He fitted his lean hips into the confined space beside her, slipping his arm around her.

Her reflexes responded immediately to the pressure and she turned a flushed face towards him. This he promptly kissed, to the delight of the assembled company.

'There's Invercargill, Max,' his grandfather pointed out, 'as it was in the first decade of this century. Dee Street, as wide as I remember it when I was a teenager, with the old disused horse tram tracks down its centre. Now there are shrubs and palm trees growing down the middle, dividing it into two. And see how wide Tay Street was in those days. But rough and pot-holed, not a vehicle in sight. Nowadays, its surface is better, but you can hardly see it for cars! You must take her there, grandson; she must follow in her grandfather's footsteps before you sweep her back to the northern hemisphere and marry her.'

He isn't going to marry me, Sally wanted to say, wishing she could be honest with these warm-hearted people. Max rose at the request of the visitors who had brought his book along for him to add his signature and good wishes.

'And you thought, Max,' Sally laughingly pointed out, 'that you'd escaped any more signing sessions by cancelling your schedule!'

She stood in her room that evening, looking out over the landscape as the sun was setting, preparing itself to rise on the other side of the world, where her mother and her stepfather lived. And Gerald. And Derek Winterton who, although she had broken off all professional contact, still haunted her in the daytime and sometimes terrorised her dreams.

She had told herself repeatedly that he couldn't harm her—could he?—now she had, in Max's interest, sacrificed the chance of ever joining the *Star and Journal* and fulfilling her ambition to become a journalist.

Sheep were dotted over a nearby hillside, while green fields with separating hedges stretched into the far distance, making her feel that she was back home. She would never forget this visit, this place, this experience of being, for a short but wonderful time, the fiancée of such a man as Max Mackenzie, the feeling of belonging, not just to him, but to his family and, yes, even to his country.

A sound at the door brought her sharply round. Max stood there, shoulder against the doorframe, hands pushed into his trouser pockets. His shirt was unfastened, his hair roughly dried after a shower. He had followed her into the bathroom, passing her with a mocking smile, his towel slung over his shoulder. His eyes had taken time to note with sardonic interest her half-bare shoulders as her seersucker wrap fell loosely open at the neck.

'How's your wound?' he asked now.

'Healing nicely, thank you,' she answered quickly as if that closed the subject and he could go.

He failed to take the hint. 'You don't wear the locket any more. Why not? Do you think I'll repeat the action and hurt you again?'

There was a dark intention in his eyes, which both frightened and thrilled her.

'No, I...Max,' she exclaimed, telling her heart to stop leaping like a pet in anticipation of a walk, 'you shouldn't be in here! What will your family think?'

'That we love each other. That I can't keep away from you. Don't fret, dear love,' he gave his usual faint emphasis to the words, 'as we're an engaged couple, or so they think, they would expect us to get together. They like you—they told me so.'

'Would it matter if they didn't?'

His gaze narrowed a fraction. 'Yes, it would.' His tone had altered slightly, gaining an edge that worried her.

He approached slowly, eyeing her from head to toe, and she wished her cotton nightdress were not so thin and revealing.

'But we aren't, Max. We don't really belong together, you and I. You know that as well as I do.'

'We don't? We can change that, Sally Dearlove. Right now.' He reached her, eyes inscrutable as his hands touched down on her shoulders, causing her to shiver, while his head dipped and his lips touched the plaster between her breasts. 'Kissing it better might speed up the healing process,' was his amused comment.

His amusement left him, his nostrils flaring, his eyes sensually serious. 'I want you, Sally.'

'Max.' She started trembling, afraid that if he started making love to her he would get under her skin so deeply she wouldn't ever be able to resist him again. 'Do you know what you're saying?'

He smiled tautly. 'You think I'm drunk?' He roped his arms around her. 'Maybe I am—drunk with desire. You must surely know the effect you have on a man. You're no innocent, with the picture of your boyfriend in your locket, which hangs between your breasts. I don't doubt that he knows all there is to know about you physically——'

'No!' Sally told herself she was wrong to say that, she should be saying, Yes, he's mine and I'm his. I *won't* be joined to you in that way, when Gerald and I . . . She couldn't tell such a lie, having acted a lie until she sent that letter of resignation to Derek Winterton.

'You're telling me no? That, lady, inflames a man's desires all the more. It gives him an opponent, a beautiful, desirable adversary to overcome and conquer. And,' his mouth spoke roughly against hers, 'conquer you I will, my lovely. Put your hands on me, here, on my heart. Feel it pounding? That, *dear love*, is how strong my need is, of a woman, of you . . .'

It isn't difficult, he'd said, for a red-blooded male to pretend to love an attractive woman.

Even as she did his bidding and slid her hands over the mat of hair on his chest, she reminded herself of his words. But it was no good, she loved him too much to hold herself away, declare her non-existent love for her boyfriend and bring an end to this beginning, which was what it was for her, although not for him.

He had dispensed with her cotton nightgown and pushed it aside with his foot. For the first time he was seeing her unclothed, and her skin stung under his dark surveillance, his hands following the path of his eyes and outlining her shape, running over her flesh as if she already belonged to him body and soul.

She looked longingly for tenderness, but none was there, only hard desire and masculine need. As his palms cupped her breasts and his mouth sought and played with their rosy, pouting tips, her head went back and she gasped at the pleasure he was giving her.

His hands went around her, lifting her, letting her know in intimate places that nothing would stop him now. As he came down upon her, she welcomed him with tight and clinging arms, the very heart and soul of her in the responses she gave to his arousing caresses.

His hands stroked her thighs, encroaching on to her most secret places where no man's hand had ever strayed before. Small, gasping cries came from her, as her body surrendered of its own accord to his coaxing touch.

His leg eased hers apart, his scorching desire setting fire to hers, and she knew then that there was no going back. Her body twisted and turned, not because she didn't want him—more than anything in the world she wanted to be his—but because her reflexes, her feminine instincts...more, her *love* for him...had taken over, and instilled in her a knowledge beyond her conscious mind as to how to please him and perhaps even cause him to desire her more.

He moved on to her, dominating her totally by his moulding hands and the rough passion of his kisses until she cried out her need of him. Then he took her, thrusting and vigorous...but checking himself sharply on her gasp.

'If you'd told me...' he said thickly, giving her time. Then, gently and with immense consideration, he moved within her. Instinct took over and infused her with an intuitive knowledge, and she began to match his movements with hers, the fast-increasing rhythm stirring her to the very depths of her being. She felt her lips forming his name and heard herself saying it, calling out over and over again how much she loved him.

Slowly, languorously, the fires died down and he lay with his head on her breast, his arms intimately around her. She stroked his hair, feeling the moisture on his forehead mingle with her own damp skin. He shifted and turned her into him. Only when she fitted into all the muscled lines and angles of him was he satisfied.

'We truly belong now?' she whispered. It had been meant to ring with loving confidence, but strangely it had turned itself into a question.

'Oh, yes, we truly belong now,' was his deep-throated reply, reverberating across his chest as her lips sought its roughened softness. 'Sleep now,' he directed, finding her mouth with his and kissing her so lingeringly she felt her desire stirring within her all over again.

He guessed, and his laugh rumbled against her, but he merely stroked her hair. 'You're fantastic, Sarah Dearlove! I could, I would, but, new as you seem to be to the whole experience, I won't, not tonight.'

Her appreciation for his thoughtfulness made her reach up and place a kiss on his cheek.

'So formal her lips are,' he growled playfully, 'after our bodies have become so—attached to each other.

What has this done,' he touched his mouth, 'to deserve such neglectful treatment?'

Sally laughed, shyly reaching up again and touching his mouth with hers. Plainly dissatisfied, he hauled her on to him and took the kiss over, pressing down the back of her head with his hand, invading and plundering her moistness, absorbing into him her gasps for mercy and giving no quarter until she kissed him back, then kissed him again and again.

He let her rest at last and she curled backwards against him, his hands possessively cupping her breasts. Feeling that heaven itself could not be as wonderful as this, she drifted into a deep and satisfying sleep.

Waking dreamily hours later, she found him standing beside the bed. He had showered and was bare to the waist, the mat of hair disappearing beneath the waistband of his trousers. It was as though, now they were one, he belonged in her room.

Then she awoke fully, frowning. What had she done? As one they might be, but they most surely did not belong. What had happened between them she had to regard as one of life's experiences. Lucky Sally Dearlove, she thought, to have had such a wonderful first-time lover.

Max bent down and her arms wound round him, and he placed a slow, drugging kiss on her lips which still throbbed faintly from his kisses in the night. Then reality really made an impact and, plainly to his chagrin, she pulled away, looking up at him worriedly.

'Max, how late is it?' She pushed aside the covers, then stopped, suddenly shy.

He laughed at her embarrassment and sat on the bed, lifting her hand and kissing his ring on her finger. As a gesture it was as possessive as that of a truly engaged man.

'Just as beautiful,' he commented languidly, 'naked in the morning sun, as in the moonlight. Of how many women could a man say that?'

Sally looked around for a covering, and he handed her the towelling robe slung over his shoulder 'I'll take pity, but I've seen and touched everything about you.' He leaned forward and whispered, 'You're mine. Whatever the future might hold, never forget that, Sally Dearlove.'

'Never,' she echoed, meaning it. Then her dreamy mind came fully awake and caught up with the other words he had uttered—'whatever the future might hold'. A shiver of apprehension ran through her.

Deliberately, she put them out of her mind. Whatever they might mean, she would not let them spoil her happiness now. As she pulled on the robe and swung her legs to the side so that she was seated beside him, he remarked, taking her by the chin and bringing her face round.

'Your first time. Uncharted waters for you. How so, Sarah?'

She shrugged, tracing the carpet's pattern. 'The circumstances at home. I did tell you about them.'

'Caring for your parents, which limited your personal freedom?' She nodded, and he added, 'I must admit to not being sorry there was no one before me.'

She looked at him sharply. 'But, Max, it's not as though we're really. . .'

His mouth met hers, silencing her. Their eyes entangled in a warmly reminiscent look, and Sally felt a glow of happiness sweep over her.

After breakfast, they wandered in the garden hand in hand, admiring the late summer flowers. Sally revelled in the sun's warmth, which came from out of a deep blue sky, forgetting the faint chill of approaching autumn that had greeted her earlier through the opened window.

Back home, spring would be showing signs of its imminent arrival.

The moment she had appeared for breakfast, Sally knew that Max's Aunt Delia had noted the radiance. That lady had smiled, glanced at her nephew, whose good humour was apparent to whoever glanced his way, and kept her own counsel.

Seated by the pool, Max pushed Sally back and hovered over her, a finger tracing her features and trailing across her throat.

'Is this,' she asked croakily, so moved by her love for him, 'a prelude to drawing me, or to throttling me?'

His answering smile was enigmatic. 'I leave you to be the best judge of that.'

Her ears detected an underlying note of seriousness and her heart jumped with fright. What did he mean? But her fears melted away beneath the impact of his slightly cruel kiss.

As she surfaced, gasping, reaching up to tug in loving revenge at a lock of his thick dark hair, there came a rustle from the undergrowth on the other side of the low hedge which formed the boundary of the land belonging to Totara Lodge.

'A wild animal?' asked Sally, smiling, still in the sun-drenched haze in which she had been moving from the moment Max had begun to make love to her the night before.

There was no smile in Max's eyes; they were diamond-hard. 'You could say that,' he answered, tight-lipped, springing up and moving fast towards the sound.

Alarmed, Sally followed, coming to a frightened halt as Max rammed open a gate in the hedge and pounced on the man who had been hiding there, pulling him up by the collar. With a sinking heart, she recognised the interloper. It was Stewart Mellidge from the *Evening Rocket* whom Max was shaking like a dog a slipper.

'Get out of my life, Mellidge,' Max was hissing through gritted teeth, 'or I'll sue the last coin out of you, and the rotten rag you represent!'

Releasing the dishevelled man, he stared into the near distance. 'Who's that louse there running for his life?' he demanded.

'The——' Stewart Mellidge needed to clear his throat. 'The photographer. He's taken one or two——'

'If your editor publishes any photographs of Miss Dearlove or myself—correction, *and* myself—I'll tear you professionally into little pieces!' snarled Max. 'And if any such shots are syndicated round the world, as, knowing the Press as well as I do, I guess they might be, I'll make it so that you, and your photographic friend, won't get another media job anywhere. Is that clear?'

The reporter tried to put his clothes to rights. 'I was only carrying out instructions, Mr Mackenzie.' A weak smile creased his worried face. 'Hi, Sally.'

He was, Sally realised, only trying to ingratiate himself with one of the two people he had been sent to snoop on, but it seemed Max didn't see it like that.

An icy stare swung her way, then left her shivering as it turned its deep-freeze self back to its main opponent.

'Don't blame me, Mr Mackenzie,' Stewart Mellidge whined. 'I was only doing my job. My editor wanted the story on you and her and—and others, for home and overseas use. *She* knew through her own editor——'

'I didn't, I swear I didn't!' Sally heard herself shriek in frightened outrage.

'So,' Max took him up, ignoring Sally's denial, 'even you knew she was an undercover journalist?'

Sally went cold. How, she wondered, could she even begin to deny such an accusation when, at the start of her acquaintance with Max, it had been true?

'Him—Hanks Filliton,' Stewart nodded towards the path his colleague had taken, 'she spoke to him the other evening at that fan's party. He told me.'

'If I did, then it was only because I thought he was a Mackenzie fan like all the others,' Sally answered, her voice still high, furious at being so deeply implicated in something of which she was entirely innocent, 'and wanted his books signed. I swear, Max, I knew absolutely n-nothing about him,' she added imploringly, her voice faltering, but on this point it appeared that he was inexplicably more inclined to believe the reporter than the woman he had made love to so wonderfully only a few hours before.

'No?' was the glacier-cold response. 'You followed him out—I watched you. One glance at his clothes, plus a quick monitoring of his whole demeanour, was sufficient for me to guess not only his calling, but the reason for his presence there.'

His attention swung back to the reporter. 'Get out, Mellidge, and if I see your whinging face again in this vicinity, or in any other way in close proximity to me and mine, I won't be responsible for what I might do to you or to any of your clique who might be with you!'

Me and *mine*, he'd said, Sally noted, her heart pounding with a foolish hope.

'But you used to be a journalist, Mr Mackenzie,' Mellidge pressed his case, 'so you must know how it is.'

Max Mackenzie was not to be moved.

Giving up, head sucked down between his shoulders, the reporter did the author's bidding and got out, his feet trailing like those of a scolded schoolboy.

Watching the young man's ears-down, tail-down exit, Sally found it in her almost to wish he hadn't gone. Now the full force of the Mackenzie anger would descend upon her. How could she bear being thrown to the verbal

lions, survive the headlong descent into the dark abyss
after reaching the heights and treading cloud as she had
been doing ever since last night when Max had made
such passionate love?

CHAPTER EIGHT

MAX swung round to face her.

'Do you really credit me with such inferior intelligence,' he rasped, his dark gaze castigating her, 'as to think I haven't had my suspicions all this time about what you've been up to?'

Oh, God, Sally thought, he *knew*? She shook her head, about to deny his accusation, but checked herself, admitting silently that any denial would be dishonest.

'What—what are you saying?' she asked, hoping against hope that he had some other, minor misdemeanour in mind. She gazed up at him, loving his face, recalling even now how in the night she had thrilled to the exquisite seduction of his touch, to the commanding strength in his limbs, remembering her rapturous responses to his thrusting, earth-shaking possession.

The wind whispered through the trees, the picture windows looked inquisitively down at them from the house, and Sally wondered sadly what had happened to her happiness since, half an hour earlier, she had stepped out into the sunlight, hand in hand with the man she loved.

'I'm saying,' that man was now enunciating each word clearly, 'that I suspected early on the true reason for your sudden appearance in my life, that you'd feigned the loss of your bag and money so as to ingratiate yourself with me.'

'That's not true, not true!'

But he had closed his mind to any defence of her actions that she might offer.

'I suspected all along,' he went on relentlessly, 'that your tripping up at the airport was no accident. At first, I was convinced that you were a fan, finding a novel way of infiltrating my personal space, but I never guessed, even then, who you really were, what you really represented. That realisation came later.'

Sally mauled her lower lip. How could she defend herself when, at the start of their acquaintance, what he was saying was correct?

'I gave you plenty of chances to admit to the true situation,' he persisted. 'When I found that *class lecture*, so-called, that you'd written about me and so carelessly gathered up with my script, why weren't you honest with me then? Why didn't you tell me it was a piece for the *Star and Journal*?'

She drew in a ragged breath. He even knew the name of the newspaper?

'When Winterton phoned and I took the call——' he was like a lawyer mercilessly presenting his case to the court '—why did you pretend he was another boyfriend, instead of telling me that he was a newspaper editor wanting his pound of flesh, the articles you'd promised him?'

She couldn't tell him the truth—that, loving him as she had come to do, she hadn't confessed because it would have meant being thrown out of his life, never seeing him again, and that she couldn't have faced. Even less could she face it now, but she had to find some kind of answer, no matter how feeble it sounded to him.

'I—maybe because I wanted to see the world——'

'At someone else's expense?' he cut in, eyes glittering with—surely it couldn't be hatred? Her very silence seemed to goad him. He seemed to interpret it as evidence that he had truly hit on the truth.

'A gold-digger all along, were you, masquerading behind a hard luck story of a financially hard-pressed young woman devoted to her ailing parents and watching sadly as her uneventful youth slipped by?'

'That was all true,' Sally protested miserably.

'Do you expect me to believe *anything* you say now I've encountered the true you?' he demanded coldly.

The true 'me', she longed to reply, was there in your arms last night, the warm, rejoicing person you made love to, and who loved you back with such abandon.

'I suppose,' she said despondently, 'the contents of my locket were another clue?'

'Too true. There were many pieces to the jigsaw, and each, I discovered, fitted neatly together. There was something else you forgot, yet which I spotted at once.'

She was too unhappy now to display interest.

'The cost of your fax calls back to your editor.'

It was true, she had forgotten. So that was how he had discovered Derek Winterton's name. Not *my* editor, she wanted to shout, but what, she asked herself, would have been the use? There was a gleam of hope... 'Didn't that prove to you that I wasn't the professional journalist you seem convinced I am?' she asked.

'No. Just a careless one.'

'Would you believe me if I told you I faxed a letter to Derek Winterton telling him not to expect any more articles or reports from me about you? Also, I did that in spite of the fact that, in doing so, I knew I was ending my career as a journalist before it had even begun, because he'd promised me, when I—I offered to—to send him articles about you——'

Oh, heavens, she thought, I've done it now! His gaze tore her to shreds.

'Which I admit I did, when I first met you,' she confessed, 'because he'd said that if I did so, I could have the job on his paper that I'd begged him to give me, a job as a journalist which I'd longed for for years.'

'What a sob story,' Max returned stonily. 'Have you got that letter? Or even a copy?'

In her haste, she recollected, choking inwardly with misery, she had torn up the letter in case, as before, she carelessly left it mixed in with Max's typewritten sheets. Which was exactly why she had not made a copy either. And heaven knew what Derek had done with his.

'I'm sorry.' She shook her head. 'There's only my word.'

Max's response was a smile that was so cynical and twisted, she felt ill inside. Her word was clearly of no use to him any more. But she had to try one more time.

'That phone call from him——' Max's eyebrows arched sardonically, as if he were willing to listen, but not to believe. 'He was probably ringing to try to persuade me to change my mind and carry on working for him.'

'Probably—that's the key word. More *probably* to get some hot copy out of you for his latest edition without the time-lag of posting it. Or even faxing it at the wrong end of the day for immediate publication.'

Sadly, Sally turned away, sighing. 'Since you refuse to accept any explanation I try to make——'

'Don't you mean excuses?'

'So your mind's inflexible. Max,' her brown eyes appealed to his, 'what about last night? It was wonderful, Max. You—you were just great, almost as if you...'

'Don't fool yourself,' he answered cruelly. 'I had a beautiful, *willing* woman in my arms. What man wouldn't take full advantage of the offer she was making me?'

Her last hope, slender though it was, had gone. All that beautiful lovemaking—it had meant nothing to him. Bitterly she recalled again what he had said about it not being difficult for a man to pretend to love an attractive woman.

'I'll get out of your life, Max. Or,' she swung round, aroused now in her own defence, 'should I say *Mr Mackenzie* now?' She turned away, quickening her step, but he halted her, his hand grasping her shoulder painfully.

'Where are you going?' he demanded.

'Where do you think? To pack and go back home.'

'Oh, no, Miss Dearlove. We have some unfinished business to attend to, and, as I've said before, I always like to finish what I start. You gave me your word—for what that's worth—to maintain this *pretence* of being lovers,' oh, she thought, how that emphasis hurt, 'until such time as it was no longer applicable. It still is, and I'm keeping you to that promise.'

'It's no good. I——'

'You,' he was tight-lipped, tautly angry, 'two-timed me, which, as you know, in my book is unforgivable. The least you can do in recompense is to agree to carry on this false engagement for as long as is necessary to my integrity as an author, my publisher's reputation and my readers' good opinion, all of which I value.'

How can I, Sally asked herself despairingly, keep up the *pretence* of loving him, when in reality I do, yet knowing just how badly he thinks of me and that he'll ditch me as soon as his need of me is over?

'But,' she protested, 'we're among people we can't fool. In the circumstances, I don't really see how——' She gestured towards the house containing his family.

'No? I'll show you how.' Before she could take a breath his arms slammed her against him and her mouth was imprisoned in a long and punishing kiss. The whimpers that escaped her throat seemed only to incense him the more, and his teeth made cruel contact, forcing from her a shuddering sob.

'That's how,' he rasped, letting her go at last, and obviously moved not one atom by the tears that spilled down her cheeks.

Pulling a handkerchief from her trouser pocket, Sally scrubbed at her face, then held it to her throbbing mouth.

'Now,' he held out his hand, 'walk with me.'

Slowly, against her will, yet conversely longing for the loving contact, she lifted her hand to meet his. They walked back towards the house and, glancing covertly at him, she saw that the frightening mask that had been his face had softened to that of a lover with his beloved. How she envied him his acting ability!

There was fight in her yet. 'If you expect *me* to follow your example, forget the past few minutes and look and act as though I love you, then——'

He stopped again, turning her and gathering her tenderly into his arms. 'Sally,' he whispered, the warmth in his eyes switched on to full power, '*dear love*, kiss me.'

And, as he had ordered, yet angry with herself for doing so, she succumbed to the charm she had not been able to resist from the moment she had met him, even standing on tiptoe, reaching up and rooting with her mouth for his.

For a few tormenting seconds he deliberately eluded her lips, then he stilled and allowed her to catch them. He tolerated the lightness of her touch for only a few seconds, then took over the kiss, his mouth coaxing and seeking, and, she found, her legs turning to water, totally irresistible.

Holding her away, he looked into her face, seeing rebellion there at his power to arouse and excite her, but mixed with a willing surrender too, and he laughed softly.

'That's better,' he growled, sliding his arm around her waist, walking her past the pool and into the house.

* * *

There was the sound of unfamiliar voices, with that of a small child raised excitedly.

Max stiffened, his arm dropping away, his expression undergoing a frightening change. He looked serious and angry and exasperated all at once. Taking in one stride the steps up to the wooden platform, he went into the house, leaving Sally to follow.

With a feeling of trepidation and a curious sense of foreboding, she stepped into the living-room.

'Max, Max!' the small child squealed as if a toy she had longed for had just been handed to her.

But Max was staring at the woman who stood across the room, beautiful and slim and pale, returning his stare, and Sally was sure that no one else existed in that room for either of them. In those few moments, she felt even more shut out of Max's life than she had from her mother's when Edith Dearlove had married Jeffrey Welling and gone to the north of England to live with him, leaving her daughter alone for the first time in her life.

'Max, Max!' the little girl exclaimed again. A fair-haired child of about three, she had broken the spell, and was swept high into his strong arms. She proceeded to hug his neck so tightly, he pretended to gasp, protesting that Merry was doing her best to suffocate him.

Never had Sally seen him so buoyant and good-humoured. He allowed the little girl to pull his hair and walk her fingers over his face, then laughed with her when she almost collapsed giggling in his arms.

It was the woman who caused Sally so much disquiet, intuition and similarity of feature telling her that she just had to be Merry's mother. Also that, beautiful as the woman was, and judging by the way she stared back at Sally as if she would like to push her down the steps and into the pool, she just had to be Francine Anderley, Max's ex-fiancée.

'Sally,' Max put Merry down, 'this is Francine Anderley. Francine——' the woman's unfriendly gaze switched to Sally '—Sarah Dearlove, my fiancée.'

Sally stared at him. He was continuing the pretence even in front of his ex-wife-to-be? Forcing a smile to meet Francine's gracious nod, she guessed the reason why Max was continuing that pretence. He must have informed Francine in advance of the falseness of his engagement, so as to avoid letting his aunt and grandfather know the truth.

'Congratulations, Miss Dearlove. Or,' with an unsmiling glance at Max, 'should I congratulate the man? I believe that it's correct etiquette to do so.'

It indeed seemed that Francine had been let into the secret.

Swallowing the jealousy that welled up painfully, Sally tore her eyes from the woman's undoubted attractions and smiled at the little girl.

'Hi there,' she said, crouching down to the child's height, 'so you're Merry. It's so nice to meet you.' She held out her hand and the little girl glanced at it uncertainly. She looked up first at her mother, whose face was wooden, then at Max, from whose expression she seemed to take some courage, and put her own hand, her left, into Sally's.

Tentatively she touched one of the large loops that swung from Sally's ear. 'Like my mummy's,' she remarked.

Except, Sally thought, that your mother's is probably made of gold, whereas mine is only gilt.

'When you grow up,' Sally asked with smile, 'will you wear earrings like your mummy?'

Merry nodded, glancing at her mother, then back. 'You're pretty,' she offered, 'like my mummy.'

'Thank you, Merry,' Sally responded with a smile, thinking, but your mother's hair is golden fair, whereas mine is dark. And it's becoming plain to me, by the way he's staring at her, that the man towering above the two of us much prefers blondes to brunettes.

Oh, Merry, Sally thought, rising and swallowing her sadness, was I really so happy when I awoke this morning that I felt I could out-sing the birds in the air?

The little girl smiled, as if she had guessed the dark-haired lady's distress, and tugged her towards the glass door.

'That's right, Merry,' Aunt Delia approved, 'take Sally into the garden,' and followed them out.

The little girl danced around the pool, heeding Sally's warnings about not going too near the edge. Max's grandfather joined them and took Merry's hand, leading her, still chattering, across to the table and chairs which stood to one side of the tiled area around the pool.

'I have to be honest with you, Sally,' Aunt Delia confided, lowering her voice. 'The main reason for Max's coming to New Zealand was a personal one. He intended mixing business with——' she hesitated '—I can't honestly say with pleasure, because things have turned out so differently from what we all envisaged.'

She lowered her voice still more. 'I'm still not clear how you two met, and it's really none of our business, but you see,' she seemed to be trying to find the most tactful words, 'he had asked us to arrange this meeting with Francine so as to judge—or so we assumed—whether or not he and she might come together again. Oh, dear, I see I've shocked you. Sit down, Sally dear. You've gone quite white.'

She drew up a chair and insisted that Sally seated herself.

'Don't take it to heart, Sally. As things have turned out, their meeting now can't have any significance whatsoever. You just have to believe that. He's chosen *you* as his wife-to-be, not Francine. I told you how much he talked about you on the phone. But you see, we couldn't tell Francine, "Don't come now, because Max has found himself another fiancée." We had to let this meeting between them take place.'

She doesn't know, Sally thought despondently, nobody knows the true situation between myself and Max, that I have no claim on him at all. Nor does she know that, when we get back home, we'll go our separate ways. That is, *if* Max returns with me. Might he not stay here, and take up with Francine where they left off? And whose child is Merry? *Max's and hers?*

Sally did not know how she got through the rest of the day. That evening, Merry seemed to sense her inner distress, and climbed on her knee and talked incessantly, bringing magazines to her so that they could discuss the photographs and pictures.

'That's good, that's fine,' Sally complimented her as Merry remembered names and places. 'You're a very intelligent little girl.'

Slowly, Sally became aware of the pause in the general conversation. Embarrassed, she glanced around. Grandfather was looking fondly at Merry and Aunt Delia looked as proud as if she herself had received the praise.

Max's narrowed eyes were on her, Francine's also, cold and calculating.

'That's your considered opinion, Miss Dearlove?' she asked, revealing not even a flicker of maternal pleasure on hearing Sally's comment. 'As a teacher, which I understand you are?' Francine regarded Sally frostily. 'Even if I hadn't been told, I would have guessed. It's written all over you—the touch of the chalk, I think it's called.' She carried out a quick, down-putting survey of Sally's outfit. 'Teachers carry their slightly despotic, faintly patronising manner around with them. Don't you agree, Max?'

Flushing angrily, Sally put Merry gently but firmly aside and stood up. 'Will you excuse me, Aunt Delia, Grandfather. Max.' She tagged on his name as if it were an afterthought, completely ignoring the woman who had insulted her. 'I have letters to write. To my mother, my friends...' Her smile softened as it rested on Merry, who ran over to her and hung on to her hand.

'I want to watch you write, Sally. Will you show me how?'

'Merry, come here!'

Reluctantly, lip quivering, the child obeyed her mother.

For some time, Sally stood at the window of her room, watching the fading light and wondering at what tactful point she could make her exit from Max's family and, above all, Max's life. Pleasant and welcoming though they had been, she felt she had no place there now.

Now Francine had appeared on the scene, it was her own cue, surely, to leave the stage, take up her backpack and the route she had abandoned and forget all about the man she had come to love more than any other person in the world.

A feeling of homesickness swept over her and she closed her eyes, imagining her mother's face. She had nursed her mother through the terrible period after her father's death. Eventually, with the arrival of Jeff Welling in their lives, the smiles had returned to her mother's face.

Now what she wanted most of all was to unburden herself to her mother's sympathetic ears, tell her the truth, putting her right about her true relationship with Max Mackenzie... whatever that might be now, after what had happened between them last night, and the arrival this morning of his one-time fiancée.

Reaching for the phone, Sally paused, holding the receiver. Was there any real need yet to confront her mother with the unhappy facts, taking the smile from her face when it had taken so many years to put it back there? If she did, wouldn't it be only for her own selfish reasons, shifting her heartache on to her mother's shoulders merely to relieve herself of her own despair?

'So you had letters to write?' Max queried scathingly from the doorway.

Sally replaced the receiver and swung round. 'I was going to call my mother.'

Max advanced, menace in his every step. 'Don't you mean the *Star and Journal*, specifically its editor, Derek Winterton? To pass on to him the latest titbits about one Maximilian Mackenzie, and the return into his life of his ex-fiancée?'

'No, I don't to the first question. And, as I've already told you, that's all behind me. I told Mr Winterton that I was opting out of that project——'

'Don't you mean,' Max repeated with barbed wire in his voice, 'to let him know in a roundabout way that although you wanted out of the Mackenzie story, you also wanted, come what may, to preserve the contract you signed with him?'

'There wasn't a contract to preserve.'

'You mean it was all settled on a verbal basis?'

Sally shrugged shoulders that felt as if they were weighted with lead, his interrogation wearying her beyond words. 'Maybe it was.'

'Who dreamed up this project—a teacher's expression—as you call it? Derek Winterton?'

By the rapier sharpness of Max's tone, Sally felt certain there was a growing intention in him of taking some kind of punitive legal action against the *Star and Journal*'s editor. Fearful of the consequences should he do so, she decided that the only course left to her was to tell him the truth, regardless of the effect it might have on his already low opinion of her.

Lifting her head high, readying herself to take whatever censure might come her way, she answered truthfully, 'I did.'

'Before you met me, or after?'

Sally moistened her lips, but held his furious gaze. 'Before. It was when I asked, unsuccessfully as it happens, to be given a job on the paper. And——' she took a breath in the face of his almost unbearable anger, '—and after, when I rang Derek Winterton from the airport, to say I'd met you quite by accident and could I now please have that job—and the Mackenzie story?'

'Coming clean now, are you? Was it then that he gave you the assignment?'

'He didn't completely commit himself, but he subsequently told me that if I gave him the kind of copy he wanted, when I returned home he'd create a job for me on the *Star and Journal*.'

Max let out a growling expletive wrapped around with a curse.

'So the little informer's being honest at last!'

'Max,' Sally choked, 'that was all before I really knew you, got involved with you...'

'And after you did—become involved, I mean—are you trying to tell me that you didn't send in any more articles about me?'

'No, Max, I——' She looked away. Oh, heavens, she thought, the evidence against her really was piling up now! 'I did. But, as you could see from the one you found, it was full of praise for you.'

'It makes not an atom of difference,' he returned icily. 'You provided copy for a newspaper about me. For that, you deserve... My God, what don't you deserve?' His jaw thrust forward and he raked her slender form with a gaze which she could almost swear left scratch marks on her skin.

Under the lash of his fury, Sally flinched. Did he, she wondered miserably, really hate her that much? She turned away, but he reached out and spun her back.

'I suppose he asked for all the intimate details—whether I used aftershave...' his hands curled round her upper arms, bruising her '—whether I liked my women submissive or truculent, *how I made love*?'

She closed her eyes, forcing herself to bear the pain so as not to give him the satisfaction of knowing that he was right, and also how much he was hurting her—both inwardly and physically.

'I can see I've hit the nail head-on. And,' he shook her, 'having now experienced a night of my lovemaking, you were about to call him,' he nodded towards the phone, 'to give him all the prurient and sordid details he wanted?'

Her eyes sprang open. 'No, I tell you! I was going to phone my mother——'

'So why did you nearly jump out of your skin and drop the phone as if it was a hot potato when I caught you at it?'

Because whatever I do now, I feel guilty. Because I know in the past I haven't acted on the level where you're concerned, but I did try to put matters right with my faxed letter to Derek, although I know you don't believe that I sent such a letter...

And now, she went on thinking, with Stewart Mellidge's lying implications about her, plus her own confession of duplicity, even though she had abandoned the role of reporter back in Auckland, she felt terrible inside, loving Max as she did.

All she said, with a shrug, was, 'I suppose my—my nerves are on edge.'

'So,' his mouth twisted, 'you've discovered it doesn't really suit your nature being a *spy*?'

She winced at his bluntness. A voice inside her was crying out, Have you forgotten last night? Did it really mean so little to you—did *I* mean so little to you—that you can put all the kisses, the exquisite intimacies, out of your mind as though they never happened?

'I think,' she went on bravely, tugging at his ring, 'you'd better find someone else to be your assistant, not to mention your so-called fiancée. I keep telling you that, way back, I opted out of the Max Mackenzie story, although I know you still don't believe I have. Well, now I'm opting out of Max Mackenzie's life. I've decided not to continue with my travels. I'm going home. So when you resume your lecture tour——' She held the ring out.

With a sinking heart, she watched him accept it. He slipped it into his pocket.

'The tour's off,' he said shortly. 'I'm returning to base too.'

'But why? There's no need for you to disappoint your readers.'

'I've cancelled the remainder of my schedule over here.'

'So it's true, then,' she exclaimed, secretly aghast, 'that you're getting together again with Miss Anderley, as your aunt thought might happen? And all the time, *you* were pretending,' she stormed, 'you used *me* as a cover, to hide your true intentions from the Press. Not only that, you used our mock engagement to make your ex-fiancée jealous, so as to bring her back to you . . .'

He clutched her upper arms and dragged her against him, his eyes tearing her apart. 'Shut that beautiful mouth of yours, Miss *Dearlove*,' he grated, 'before you do as much damage with your nasty innuendoes as your unscrupulous use of *me* has done!'

He threw her from him, dusting his hands as if they had been defiled.

'By the morning,' he informed her coldly, 'I'll have made new plans.' Again he raked her from head to foot. 'You will be in them. I haven't finished with you yet. Sleep well, Miss Dearlove...if your conscience lets you!'

CHAPTER NINE

IT WAS not her conscience that kept Sally from sleep, it was Max's refusal to believe that she was no longer playing at being a journalist. What else, she asked herself bluntly, had she been doing but acting the role of an *amateur* sleuth? She'd had no training.

So, she thought restlessly, she was literate and could write a good letter, could even concoct articles for teachers' journals, not to mention the occasional women's magazine. And yes, she could *teach* people to write, which was what she had been trained for. But act like, think like, *write* like a journalist? Never!

At which honest, if self-disparaging, revelation, she tossed and turned yet again, longing for the morning, yet knowing it was only just past midnight.

If only, her thoughts went in circles, Max would believe her. If only she'd kept a copy of that letter she had sent to Derek... Throwing aside the covers, she pushed her feet into slippers and wrapped her robe around her.

The floorboards creaked as she crept along to Max's room. What she had to tell him might—just—restore his trust in her. It was worth a try. Wasn't it? But even as she tapped on his door, she wished she had waited until morning. The moment the door opened, she wondered if Francine was there and she'd interrupted...

'What do you want?' Could his tone have been more unwelcoming? Not only that, he was keeping her standing there. Did that mean he couldn't tolerate her near him any more? Or was there another, more likely reason, one—or someone—that he wanted to hide?

'Please, I——' She shook her head. 'It can wait.'

His hand reached out and pulled her in. The door closed quietly behind her. Not only was the bed empty, it was undisturbed. So he'd had difficulty sleeping too? Or had he been wrestling with the problem of whether or not to resume his loving relationship with Francine?

'What the hell's going on in that mind of yours?' he derided. He must have noticed where her glance had rested. 'Did you honestly think that tonight I'd taken yet another woman into my bed? What kind of a louse do you think I am?'

'No, Max, I——' But the idea had been in her mind! 'I had to see you to——'

'You came to snoop, just in case I had? And if so, were you going to call your editor and give him the lowdown—and I do mean "low"—on my gluttonous sexual appetite, and how my immoderate libido forces me to seduce a different woman every night?'

Sally sought his eyes, finding in them only censure and contempt. 'Please... will you give me a hearing?'

He was silent, his hands finding the pockets of his black loose-hanging robe. His unshaven appearance in the subdued lighting made him mysterious and, in his present mood, darkly menacing.

She longed to reach up and run her fingers down his cheeks, trace the grooves around his jaw, unpleat the frown between his eyes. All of which he had allowed her to do the night before, laughter lighting his eyes as she had done so, then rolling her over and forcing her hands above her head as he took her mouth in a deeply invasive kiss.

'When we do get back,' she said at last, taking his silence as consent, 'I'll be able to *prove* to you that I wrote to Derek Winterton telling him that I was opting out of this story. Not only that, that he'd get no more copy from me about you. Max,' as the scepticism did not shift from his eyes, 'on my honour I *swear* that's what I did, that I'm speaking the truth.'

'So,' was he softening at last? 'you're claiming that you'll be able to produce the evidence on our return?'

'I'm claiming that, Max.'

He seemed to relent and lifted her chin. 'I accept your statement. From this moment, until the evidence you're so sure you'll have is placed in front of me, I shall suspend my disbelief—you remember?—and agree to a truce. Which we'll seal with this.' He went to a drawer and extracted the ring, pushing it securely back on her finger. 'And this.'

He pulled her into his arms. 'What is it about you,' he muttered almost angrily, 'that I can't...?' His mouth lowered slowly, tantalisingly. When it met hers there was an explosion inside her of longing to feel his hard body beside hers, offering her his strength and his passion, and afterwards the rest which she had been unable to find until she had sought and secured his trust in her again.

There was a laugh deep within him, and his arms wrapped her against him, letting her feel his hardening body. 'I know how it is with you,' he murmured against her ear, 'as with me, but the answer's no. I might be too hard on you, even cruel to you, if I made love to you tonight.' Sally endeavoured to free herself, colouring deeply, embarrassed beyond words at her own betrayal of her feelings.

Max held her easily, enjoying her struggles, pulling her against him and pushing aside the neckline of her nightdress, lowering it until the burgeoning shape of her spilled over. He kissed each breast, using his tongue to caress and excite, then transferring his lips once again to hers in a long and drugging kiss, his own chest, now bare and exposed, crushing the curving softness of hers.

'Sleep now, Sarah,' he said gruffly, easing her away, 'in your own bed tonight.'

His tone was decisive, but his eyes held a strange and puzzling glow.

Merry met her with a little squeal of pleasure at the foot of the stairs next morning.

'Take me to the pool,' she commanded, grabbing Sally's hand. 'Grandpa says I mustn't go there without someone with me.'

'Hi, Merry.' Sally lowered herself to the child's height. 'I love the big bow in your hair. It matches your pretty blue dress.'

'Think hard about it, Francine,' Max's voice carried from behind the closed living-room door. 'There's got to be a decision. For Merry's sake, you can't go on like this. It won't be easy, you know that and so do I, but there's a way round the difficulties, every one of them.'

Sally rose, her breath catching on the knife-sharp thrust of pain that had bit into her. The word 'it' could only mean one thing—he was persuading her to take the vital step and go back to him.

So this was heartache, this was what total rejection felt like. There was everything false about their engagement, but, Sally thought, gritting her teeth, there was nothing false about this terrible feeling that had her by the throat.

Max wanted Francine back in his life, that much was clear. Last night, of course, he had not wanted her, Sally Dearlove, because she had been the *wrong woman*. How could she have been so foolish as to give away her need of him like that?

'Sally?' Merry, frowning and worried now, had been watching her. 'Take me outside, please?'

'I don't know,' Francine was saying slowly. 'I have things to work out. I need time, Max...'

There was a short silence, during which Merry tugged at Sally's hand. Sally knew she should not be listening, but something overpowered her common sense and kept her there.

'So,' Max sounded resigned now, 'I'll take Merry at least.'

Yes, Sally thought as their voices lowered, Merry would be the link, the insurance policy to make certain that her mother eventually followed, joining Max and— *their* daughter?

'Well now,' Aunt Delia bustled towards them, 'have you found an escort, young lady, while Grandfather and I get the breakfast?' She cast a worried look towards the living-room, but changed it into a smile. 'Did you sleep well, Sally?'

'I did,' Merry chipped in, relieving Sally of the trouble of answering. After leaving Max, she had lain restlessly awake until dawn.

The living-room door opened and Merry squeaked an ecstatic, 'Max! Take me to the pool. Sally's busy talking.'

Max smiled down at the eager little girl, then exchanged a glance with his aunt. 'Grandfather will take you, dear,' Aunt Delia said, as the older man advanced, hand extended to take Merry's. Chattering, she went with him willingly.

'Sally, I'd like a word.' Max was so serious that there was no way that she could refuse, and she followed as he had known she would.

He passed the closed living-room door and made his way to the playroom. Toys were scattered everywhere. Even the two chairs, one of which was a child's size, were piled with them.

'I'll free this one,' said Max, but Sally had picked up a teddy bear from the low child's chair, swept aside the remaining clutter and lowered her slender self tightly into it, holding the toy bear on her knee.

Max allowed himself a brief smile as, quite unselfconsciously, she smiled up at him. 'Your normal milieu?' he commented. 'As a teacher, I guess, you're accustomed to this kind of environment?'

'My students are way up here,' she used her hand to indicate height.

'Their toys are rather more sophisticated?'

She returned his smile. 'Somewhat.'

'So you teach——'

'Correction. Used to teach.'

His eyes darkened and Sally cursed herself for reminding him of her change of occupation, which he plainly believed she still followed, despite her repeated denials.

'So you taught,' he went on, 'an older age group.'

She nodded. 'Whenever their adolescent problems and their psychological hang-ups allowed me, plus coping with their resistance to learning if they weren't properly motivated.'

'But they liked you, and because of that they did listen and learn?'

She coloured, unduly pleased with the compliment implicit in his remark. He looked at her long and hard, commenting at last, 'Curious how little I know about you.' And yet we've been so intimate . . . the words hung unspoken between them.

'And,' she whispered, because there was something in the air, a tension that made her hold her breath, 'I know so little about you.' Despite, some more unspoken words were saying, your having made passionate love to me not so very many hours ago. But now it's Francine he wants, she reminded herself sharply. Hadn't she heard them talking, almost certainly discussing the future— theirs together?

Max walked about the room, carefully picking his way between miniature cars and coloured pencils and dolls

staring wide-eyed at the ceiling, all laid on for Merry—
the adored grandchild and great-niece? The thought was
too painful for Sally to contemplate.

'I'd like you to fly back with me,' he said briefly.

Her heart leapt, then subsided. This time, no doubt,
in the aircraft Francine would occupy the seat beside
him. Don't fool yourself, she thought, that it's *your*
company he wants.

'There's something else,' he added. 'I should like you
to take charge of Merry on the journey home.'

'Her mother isn't coming?'

'Francine has some personal matters to attend to, so
she's delaying her journey. I've promised to take Merry
with me to help her over this——' Sally felt that the faint
pause held some significance '—difficult patch.'

Francine was entrusting her child to Max's care? Surely
that *proved* that Max was Merry's father?

'Will you do this favour for me?' he pressed, standing
in front of her, legs like tough columns topped by hard-
boned hips and a waist which, Sally knew by experience,
was without an inch of spare flesh.

Say no, she warned herself, and she'd never see him
again. Saying yes would at least mean a delaying of the
devastating parting of the ways.

'Yes,' came from her in a whisper.

'Thanks,' Max said simply, but his eyes held gratitude—and something more? —as he eased her out of
the low chair, spilling the bear from her lap. He was
pulling her closer, eyes on her lips, when the door burst
open, and Merry rushed in shrieking as Grandfather
pretended to chase her.

Three days later they left for home. Francine had handed
her daughter into Sally's care with detailed instructions
as to her routine and her dietary needs.

As if I were being employed as Merry's nanny, Sally thought with amusement, instead of just escorting her along with Max on a plane flight. 'I want you to pass all this information on to my mother,' Francine had added imperiously.

Sally had made a secret, rueful face at Max, then realised he would not appreciate the joke since he was in love with the woman, wasn't he? To her surprise, Max had smiled. He had assured the lady that her daughter was in good hands, and never fear, that daughter, small though she was, would no doubt without hesitation inform her temporary 'parents' of her needs and wishes should they ever dare to neglect or forget them.

Aunt Delia had given Sally a final hug and, in Francine's presence, repeated in loud tones how delighted she and Grandfather were at Max's choice of a wife-to-be.

Francine had turned haughtily away and taken Max's arm, tilting her face for his goodbye kiss. Sally made for the waiting car, finding the sight of Max about to bestow that kiss unbearably painful.

The flight home, Sally found, was wearisome and long. Max spoke little, having come well supplied with books and magazines. These he read with deep concentration, frequently making notes, in between the times when he helped cope with an increasingly restless young charge.

Sally spent the journey alternately cuddling, pacifying and even chasing a sometimes rebellious Merry along the gangways, with Merry collapsing into giggles on Sally's lap. After which she would listen enthralled as Sally invented story after story.

To her embarrassment, Sally had once or twice found that Max was listening. She had halted, turning pink and looking at him askance, at which he had returned her glance with wry amusement.

'If I took an Alice-in-Wonderland pill,' he'd said once, 'and reduced myself many times in size, would you take me on your knee and tell me a story?'

'What,' she'd whispered back with mock fury, 'and have you plagiarise it from me and use it in one of your books?'

He had laughed loudly at this, head back, and Sally felt a ripple of happiness go through her that she had been able to bring about a lightening of his so far dauntingly serious mood.

He had told her that, on leaving the airport, they would drive to his house in Surrey where they would spend the night. 'Tomorrow,' he added, 'I'll take Merry to Francine's mother. She's willingly agreed to look after her little granddaughter.'

At which point, Sally warned herself, she would be free to fill her backpack with her belongings and her foolish love, leave behind all the things that had been bestowed on her as the celebrated author's so-called fiancée and bow gracefully out of his life.

Mid-March, which had been so warm and pleasant in New Zealand, struck without mercy sun-indulged skin and too-lightly clad bodies as the passengers spilled out of the aircraft and made their teeth-chattering way towards Customs.

'Why is it so cold?' Merry asked plaintively, shivering in her fleecy-lined jacket and wool trousers.

Sally, who carried Merry while Max dealt with the luggage, asked, 'Hasn't she been to the northern hemisphere before?'

'She was born here, then taken south, but yes, she's revisited with Francine, but she was too young on those occasions for the seasonal and temperature difference to register.'

He knew the child's past history so well, not to mention that of her mother, Sally reasoned, trying hard to be objective, he just *had* to have a closer relationship with Merry than merely that of her mother's ex-fiancé and lover.

Relatives and friends meeting the new arrivals waved and smiled, heaving cases from airport trolleys and leading the way to whatever transport awaited them.

'Isn't there anybody,' Merry asked, still safe in Sally's arms and glancing round a little sadly, 'waving to us? Yes,' she squeaked, pointing, 'there!'

'Where?' Max asked sharply. A series of flashes made Merry turn her face into Sally's hair. 'My God,' he ground out, 'the rat-pack!'

He made for a gap in the crowds, but the reporters—there were two of them—and photographer followed.

'Over here, Mr Mackenzie,' one of them urged. 'Oh, come on, give us a break!'

'We're only doing our job,' said the other, a woman. 'Give us a quote, at least.'

Frightened, Merry clung to Sally. 'Isn't she lovely,' the man said. 'The image of you.' Which was a lie, Sally thought, if there ever was one! 'You're one of us too, Miss Dearlove, you can't deny it. We all know about your connection with the *Star and Journal*. We read your pieces about life with...'

The public address system delivered a series of messages and his words were lost. Max, having been forced to follow Sally and Merry, came on the scene, his expression dark and forbidding.

'How old's the offspring, sir? Three and a half? So the relationship's—add on a year, yes?'

'That's our business,' Sally retorted, then turned urgently. 'I'm not one of them, Max, honestly. I told you I'd broken off all contact——'

Max ignored her denial.

'A picture, Mr Mackenzie,' the photographer pleaded. 'How about a family group?'

'The child's not hers,' the woman reporter declared firmly. 'The little girl's his and his ex-fiancée's. I bought Derek Winterton a drink and he showed me the cuttings he'd kept of all the copy *she*,' a finger pointed at Sally, 'had faxed in about him.'

Sally's face drained. 'What copy? What cuttings?' she asked desperately. 'And who's *him*?'

Merry was sobbing into her neck and no one answered the questions.

The photographer urged Sally, still holding Merry, to stand beside Max. The cameras flashed once more, then the reporters stood back, watching them leave.

It was early morning and Sally, jet lagged from the long flight, having managed only snatches of sleep, was heavy-eyed and tired to her bones. Merry sat tiredly between them in the taxi, staring out wide-eyed.

Tiredness making conversation an effort, none of them spoke, except to comment on the difference between the March they had left behind, with its leaves already hinting at an autumn soon to come, and the March which, here, was giving promise of buds opening to the spring before many weeks had passed.

'Max?' Sally ventured, interrupting Max's reverie.

He had been so quiet she had concluded that he must have been thinking about his book. He hadn't, to her knowledge, touched his work since visiting his aunt. Or maybe he was brooding? About Francine, about leaving her behind? About still being burdened with one Sally Dearlove, whom he didn't know how to leave by the wayside without detracting from his public image?

'Yes?' he responded, his attention still on the passing scene.

'When shall I give you your ring back?'

A brittle pause, then, 'Why the question? You can't wait to get back to your boyfriend, unencumbered by any supposed liaison with me?'

Sally frowned. 'Boyfriend? Oh, you mean Gerald. He——' She shook her head. 'Surely you understand? If he'd been important to me, I wouldn't even have considered allowing you...let alone actually doing what we——'

'OK,' drily, 'I get your meaning. And the answer to your question is, when I want the ring back, I'll tell you.' With which, Sally told herself, she had to be satisfied.

'Is this New Zealand?' asked Merry, staring, very puzzled, through the window.

Sally did not laugh, feeling almost as disorientated as the little girl. 'No, pet,' she answered gently, 'it's England.'

The name plainly meant nothing to Merry, who asked, 'Are we going to Aunt Delia's and Grandfather's house?'

Max turned, smiling, from the window.

'No, Merry,' Sally answered again. 'Tomorrow you're going to your granny's, but today we're all going to Max's house.'

'Will Aunt Delia be there? Will——' with greater hope '—will my mummy be there?'

'No, Merry,' Max took over the question-and-answer session, 'not your mother—a lady called Ellen, Ellen Farmer, who looks after me and my house.'

Merry lapsed into silence, staring out at roofs and clouds, which Sally reckoned was all she could see from her low position on the seat. Even to Sally, it seemed half a lifetime before Max leaned forward to give the driver detailed instructions as to how to reach his house.

The taxi proceeded down a drive which curved to reveal a two-storeyed residence rising self-importantly, as well it might, Sally reflected admiringly, from lawns and shrubs and the greenery of broad-leafed trees. Constructed in rustic red brick, its many windows reflected the morning sun and from its grey-slated roof sprang a couple of dormer windows which nestled, as if for warmth, between two tall and characterful chimneys.

Merry stirred as the taxi slowed to a halt. Max lifted her down, offering Sally his hand as she stepped out, more than a little overwhelmed, her tired brain reeling a little at the impact of her new surroundings.

Was it really true, she wondered, that she hadn't known this man, apart from reading his books and newspaper reports about him, before she had met him so precipitately at Heathrow Airport? Deep down, she still felt bewildered by the change which had overtaken her life from the moment of their meeting.

Ellen extended a warm welcome, her hand taking Sally's after greeting her employer.

'I'm so glad to meet Mr Mackenzie's fiancée, Miss Dearlove,' the warmly smiling lady pronounced. 'The papers—they've been saying such things!'

'Such as?' Max queried, frowning.

'Oh,' Ellen gestured, 'like how much you love each other, and—well, you know, things like that. Oh, what a dear little girl!'

Merry was enfolded in a hug at her own level. 'There've been ever so many phone calls for you, Mr Mackenzie,' Ellen said, rising and lifting some of the cases, 'especially from your fan clubs. I'll take these up, then I'll get you a nice cup of tea. Yes, Mr Mackenzie?'

'I'm Merry,' Merry offered, tipping her head.

'Are you, love? Then that's what I'll call you. There's a lovely room been made up for you, dear, right next to Miss Dearlove's, as Mr Mackenzie told me to do when he rang all the way from the other side of the world.'

'Where's all the post?' called Max, as he turned to walk through the entrance hall.

'Stacked up in your workroom, Mr Mackenzie. There's such a lot of it! I should leave it for now, if I were you. I bet none of you got much sleep.'

'You're right, Ellen,' Sally replied, yawning. 'Especially a certain small person.'

Ellen laughed. 'Now here's your room, Miss Dearlove. Hope you like it.' She lowered Sally's cases to the peach-coloured carpet which, from a quick glance, Sally noted matched the bedspread and curtains, and went next door. 'And here's where Merry will sleep. Like it, dear? It's all pink colours and dainty frills, isn't it?'

Merry nodded and yawned, and Ellen fussed over her, opening her small case and saying, 'I'll have this unpacked in no time. Just you take her to the bathroom for a wash, Miss Dearlove, then she can have a nice sleep before lunch. You too, dear, if you know what's good for you.'

'But Mr Mackenzie——' Sally began.

'I'll take care of him,' Ellen answered with an understanding smile that gave away her romantic thoughts. 'Don't you worry. Should I bring your tea up, or——?'

'I'll skip it, if you don't mind,' said Sally 'I'm so tired, I don't think I could stay awake long enough to drink it!'

CHAPTER TEN

FOLLOWING Ellen's directions to Max's workroom, as she had called it, Sally found him in a strangely uncompromising mood.

He stood, polite but unsmiling, inviting her to sit. She chose a place on a sofa which was set at an angle to a second one in the centre of the room. A series of linked desks bore lamps, folders and reference books. On a separate table stood a mountain of unopened mail.

Glancing about her, Sally found herself liking the room and felt that she too could work there. Oddly uncommunicative, hands in pockets, Max stood at the patio doors, staring out. Looking at his back, flexed against tiredness, his profile hard and etched against the late afternoon light, Sally felt a tug of emotion that threatened to overwhelm her.

She loved him desperately, he would never know how much. The happiness she had experienced in those hours she had spent in his possessive arms kept returning to her dreams. The awful part, she had discovered, was waking up ever since to the emptiness of her bed and, worst of all, the terrible vacuum in her heart.

'Did you get any sleep, Max?' she asked, saying the first thing that came into her mind to provoke a response, *any* kind of response.

'I rested for an hour or so. It was enough.'

He had spoken abruptly, and Sally, frowning, wondered what was eating him, since it was plain that something was.

'Have you started on that great pile of mail?' she asked, attempting again to break the uncomfortable silence.

'Some of it.'

His tone had been inordinately abrupt, and Sally's heart sank. Were they back to the old enmity and distrust? As if he could not contain his anger any longer, Max swung round and confronted her, arms folded, legs aggressively apart.

The frown marks between his brows, along with his diamond-hard eyes, were intimidating enough to frighten the boldest of creatures. And Sally was feeling anything but bold at that moment.

'What cuttings,' he shot at her, 'what cuttings was that woman reporter referring to?'

So it was that that had been eating him on the taxi ride from the airport!

'If I tell you I don't know,' Sally answered, 'will you believe me? No,' despondently, 'I thought not. All the same, I'm as puzzled as you are. I can only repeat what I've told you over and over: after sending in a couple of articles—no more than school essays really, since I've had no journalistic training—I informed Derek Winterton of my decision to withdraw from our verbal agreement and——'

He jerked away, halting her flow of words, walking to his desk and back again. 'It gets monotonous. Every time someone comes out with the truth about you, you deny——'

'It's not the truth!' she cried. 'I'm the one speaking the truth. Believe me or not, as I see it, I'm up against the collusion of the Press, the "let's all stick together, boys" syndrome. For some reason, probably because you're so well known and are the central figure in it all, they've got together on this and are ganging up on me,

an inexperienced outsider, a gatecrasher, as they see it,
to the profession——'

'All very plausible—if only I were gullible enough to
accept it. The trouble is that those hints and innuendoes
about you have been repeated so often, *and on different
sides of the world*, that I find it very hard indeed to
believe you.'

'OK,' she cried, 'you're saying in a roundabout way
that ditching me is very high on your list of priorities.
Well, I'll save you the bother. It's the end, isn't it?' she
said, unable to hide the catch in her voice. 'It has to be.
I can't go on like this. I—heaven help me, I——' *Love
you,* she'd been about to tell him. She shook her head,
compressing her lips to stop them trembling, and made
for the door.

As she reached it, it was pushed open and a small
figure peered round it. 'Are we going to my granny's
house now?' asked Merry.

'Tomorrow, poppet,' Sally answered, taking a breath
and trying to keep the waver out of her voice. 'Are you
hungry? I am. It's really teatime, but the clock in your
tummy might not agree. Let's go and see, shall we, if
Ellen's cooking anything in the kitchen.' It was an ideal
chance to get away from Max's harsh and unforgiving
presence.

'She's preparing a light meal,' he informed her coldly.
'I don't know what you meant just now by "the end",
but I trust you'll stay at least until we take Merry to
Francine's mother?'

Something made her glance down. Merry was looking
up at her so anxiously, Sally realised the little girl had
sensed that all was not well between the two of them.
So until tomorrow, Sally decided, for Merry's sake, she
would play her part in attempting to maintain at least
the appearance of peace between herself and Max.

'I'll keep my promise,' she answered, and even managed a smile, bringing a relieved smile to Merry's face too.

The house was silent, the dark world outside silvered by the moon. Earlier Sally had telephoned her mother, telling her she was back and staying with Max.

'Which is just as it should be,' Edie had exclaimed joyfully. 'When are Jeff and I going to meet him, dear? Make it soon, won't you? Now you must rest, sleep off your jet lag. When you've got over that, ring again, and then we can talk about arranging a meeting. You don't know,' she added, 'how much we're looking forward to meeting our new son-in-law-to-be.'

But Sally couldn't sleep, worrying about how to persuade her mother finally to accept that her engagement to Max really wasn't genuine. Also, her body clock was telling her that her watch just had to be wrong, that it was not midnight, it was midday, and she should be up and going about her daytime business.

Merry too had found it difficult to settle down. When Sally had put her to bed, she had obediently closed her eyes, but they had sprung open almost immediately.

'I'm not tired,' she had said plaintively.

So Sally had sat patiently beside her, telling her stories until Merry's eyelids had closed and she had slept. Now Sally wished with a rueful smile that someone would sit with her and tell her stories too, so that she could drift into sleep.

Standing at the window, she stared tiredly at the gardens spread out below, then turned away to sink down on to the sofa which was set against a wall across the room.

That piece of furniture was, she reflected, a thoughtful touch, placed there no doubt for a guest who might occasionally wish to opt out of socialising, preferring instead to spend some time alone. A sound from the landing made her tense. Max had entered before she had had time to realise his intention.

'I saw the light under your door.' He stood looking down at her reclining figure, hands in his pockets, expression inscrutable. 'I came in without knocking because I reckoned that if I'd asked your permission I'd have had to wait a long time.'

'No, you wouldn't, Max...' Then she realised just what kind of an invitation had been wrapped up in her denial.

He came a little nearer and in the subdued lighting she could see the evening stubble growth shading his jaw, the shadows of fatigue unindulged beneath his eyes. His unfastened shirt hung loosely over his belted jeans. There was the mat of hair, the rough feel of which Sally remembered so well against her cheek and hotly sensitised skin.

'Internal time-keeping giving you trouble?' Max asked softly. 'You can't persuade yourself that it's sleeping time, not activity time?'

She nodded, smiling up at him. His mood was so mellow, so much warmer than it had been earlier in the day, when Merry's arrival on the scene had just prevented her precipitate exit, her hopes started climbing, her heartbeats overtaking them in great strides.

'Do you know any cure, Max,' she whispered chokily, 'for winding down the body clock when it's convinced it's a.m. and not p.m.?'

His eyelids lowered, his downward glance plainly peeling the flimsy layers from her prone figure. Sally wished he would stop, because her skin was beginning to respond madly to his visual caresses.

'There's a way,' he answered, 'that we both know of.'

She took a shallow breath. 'I——' How should she go on? I love you and want you more than anything in the

world, but . . .? 'Did——' There was a hoarseness there
and she cleared her throat. 'Why did you come?'

His eyes dipped lazily to her outstretched legs, the
provocative cleft which the low neck of her nightdress
revealed, but his tone was neutral as he told her,

'Merry's grandmother rang. She asked if it was possible for us to keep Merry with us for a while. Unfortu-
nately, she tripped and fell while out shopping recently—
hurt her leg badly, broke some bones in her ankle. She's
in plaster for three weeks or so, and consequently she's
on crutches.'

Sally frowned in sympathy. 'Did you ask if there was
anything we could do?'

'I did, but her sister's staying with her, she said,
looking after her. I assured her that Merry could live
here for as long as necessary and that, if she needed any
more help, not to hesitate to contact me.'

'Which means that you'll want me to stay on
until——'

'Until her grandmother's fit enough to take her on,
yes.' In a softer tone, he added, 'I need your help, Sally.'

'Are you sure,' she asked, bitterness creeping in, 'that
you *trust* me enough to look after Merry?'

'In this respect, I'd trust you,' was his faintly cruel
reply. 'It's plain that you love children.'

'You have to, don't you,' she answered, her gaze en-
meshing with his, her limbs turning to water at the look
in his eyes, 'to be a teacher?'

'Sally,' he said, crouching down beside the sofa,
'Sally. . .' He seemed to have caught her hoarseness.

He was pulling her towards him, finding her mouth,
parting her lips, then swinging her, holding the kiss, up
and across to the bed. 'Brazen deceiver you may be, but
God forgive me, I can't resist the woman in you,' he
muttered against her mouth.

'No, Max,' she stiffened in the face of his relentless mistrust, but she so wanted to give in to him, 'you can't, you mustn't, not now that Francine's back in your life.'

'You're the one who wears my ring,' to her bewilderment she heard him say. Was he, in these moments of very male desire, forgetting that theirs was only a mock engagement?

Whether he was or not didn't seem to matter now. Caution deserted her too, and she closed her mind to the warnings her better judgement was trying to give. Her hands reached out for him like a starving person reaching for succour. They stroked his flesh, loving the hard, muscled feel of it, remembering the joys it had brought her. As he shed his clothing and tugged her against the hard, lean length of him, she pressed her fingertips into his shoulders and covered his rough mat of chest hair with breathless, fervent little kisses.

He peeled off her nightdress and ran his hands over her heated flesh, following the path they had taken with lips that savoured and nipped and invaded the intimate valleys of her body. He was not gentle, nor had she expected him to be—hadn't he warned her at his aunt's house that if he took her when he was still in doubt of her integrity, he might be cruel and take her without mercy?

She was lost in the mists of giving and accepting, in the relentlessness of his hunger for all that she could give him, when a sound came through which she at first rejected. But something deep within her knew it was a cry for help by a small human in distress and that, whatever the sacrifice, it had to be answered.

Max must have heard it too, since he groaned and lay, head on her breasts, his chest moving with the deep, despairing inhalation of his lungs. 'Stay,' he muttered on a growling sigh.

'It's Merry, Max,' Sally whispered, 'I must go to her.'
She stroked his hair, longing to do as he commanded,
but knowing that she had to go.

'Hell,' he exclaimed against her skin, his hands still
tightly compressing her flesh, 'of all times, to choose
now!'

Gently she prised his fingers from her bruised skin
and slid from under him, pulling on her nightdress and
wrapping a robe around her still throbbing body. Don't
do this to yourself and to him, her other self cried out,
stay with him and bring your love to its true fulfilment...

The small voice in the night called out again, and Sally,
placing her tender hand against his moist and naked
back, whispered, 'I'm truly sorry, Max, but——'

'OK, go,' was his groaning answer.

A wailing cry greeted Sally as she approached Merry's
bed. 'I want my mummy,' she sobbed. 'Where's my
mummy?'

'She'll come some day soon,' Sally answered, soothing
the hot little brow, and wishing that she herself knew
the answer to that question.

In the wearying hour or so that followed, Sally forced
herself to dig deep into the creative part of her mind
and produce yet more stories for Merry's benefit. At
one time, she felt rather than heard Max enter the room.
He stood behind her as she sat on a child's chair, then,
choosing a moment when Merry's eyes were momentarily closed, he crouched behind the tiny chair and
pulled Sally back against the soft mat covering his chest.

His hands came around her, sliding in to find her bare
flesh, cupping her breasts. His cool, demanding lips
roamed around her throat, forcing her head to tilt backwards. He took a lingering kiss, then, as Merry stirred
again, demanding more stories, he broke contact and
straightened, quietly leaving them.

When, two hours later, Sally had tucked in a sleeping child and returned to her own room, finding it empty, she reproached herself for foolishly hoping that Max might be there.

Waking late, she showered and sped downstairs, finding Merry in the kitchen, 'helping' Ellen. The little girl was her usual bright self, seeming to have forgotten her restless and fretful night.

Sally assured Ellen that the toast and coffee she herself prepared was quite sufficient in the way of nourishment at that time of the day.

'Um—Mr Mackenzie, where will I find him, Ellen?' she asked with a false casualness, trying not to sound as if finding him and rushing into his arms mattered to her more than anything in the world.

'In his workroom, Miss Sally. I'll keep an eye on Merry. I warn you, dear, Mr Mac might bite your head off.' Merry put up her hands and held her own head. 'He's in one of his moods, isn't he, pet?'

Merry nodded. 'He's busy, he said. Bizzy, bizzy,' she repeated, giggling.

Sally wondered if, like Merry, she should hold on to her own head when she tentatively tapped on Max's workroom door. He swung round at her entrance and his expression was so full of barely contained menace that she felt like backing out of the room.

He had tackled the mountain of mail, the floor and every other flat raised surface being covered with it. Torn envelopes lay scattered, their enclosed letters having been either crumpled and flung to distant corners, or allowed to float discarded to cover the carpet.

Most ominous of all was the appearance of the largest desk, cleared of everything but newspaper cuttings. These were spread, with meticulous care and obvious intent, across its entire surface. Staring at them from a distance, Sally was filled with a terrible foreboding. Were these the 'cuttings' to which that woman reporter had referred and of which she, Sally, had denied all knowledge?

'Yes, Miss Dearlove,' Max rasped, 'you're so right to look hunted. These are newspaper cuttings about me, by you,' he pointed, 'with a truncated version of your name, but your byline, make no mistake. And what's their subject matter? My private life, my intimate preferences, my past, about which you know nothing, but about which you used your very fertile, if grossly *flawed*, imagination.'

'Cuttings?' Sally gasped. 'By *me*?' She shook her head. 'How——? Who——?'

'At least you're not denying their existence,' he grated. 'How did they get here? I'll tell you. Courtesy of the postal service. Who sent them? That valued fan of mine called Henni Curzon, who accosted me for my signature at Heathrow Airport. She was, she said,' he pushed a letter towards Sally, 'so incensed by the statements in these articles that she sent them to me, knowing that I would have missed their publication during my stay in New Zealand. She therefore made sure, she said, that I'd receive them without fail on my return.'

Sally took a breath, intending to declare her total ignorance of what he was talking about, but he stopped her before she could begin.

'Henni suggested,' he went relentlessly on, 'that I should start legal proceedings without delay, both against the journalist who made these scurrilous statements, and the editor of the newspaper who published them. What do you say, Miss *Dearlove*,' he snarled, 'to my suing you, not to mention your garbage-minded editor, for every penny, every cent, you each possess?'

At first, Sally struggled with the printed words. They jumbled themselves into meaningless shapes, then reassembled into the wrong order. She blinked madly in an effort to restore her ability to read straight, her stupefied brain beginning to take in the statements to which Max had referred.

They were indeed outrageous, every single one of them, and her hands shook as she pulled first one, then the other nearer so that she could read each scandalous word. They cast shocking slurs on Max's private life, insinuating that he was playing around not only with his ex-fiancée, of whose daughter, the reports stated, he was the father, but with the girl he was currently, and quite falsely, calling his 'fiancée'.

All this, the report asserted, was a ruse to cover up his resumed affair with the above-mentioned ex-girlfriend. The writer had been astute enough not to mention that lady's name. Every piece had been signed 'Sally Dear'.

Sally stood, hands on the desk, shoulders sagging, eyes closed, feeling faint. Someone, she concluded, must really hate her to have done this to her. But who? There could be only one person, and he didn't hate her. He was just a nasty-minded opportunist and probably furious with her for backing out of a good story.

Her face pale, she turned to meet the fury in Max's eyes. She could only shake her head. What would have been the use of once again denying complicity? He had already declared that it was 'getting monotonous'.

'If I show you that letter I sent to Derek Winterton,' she managed to say, 'will you read it and believe what your eyes tell you?'

'OK, produce it. *If it exists.* Until then, I'll hold off my instinct to lift that phone and call my lawyer.'

Sally couldn't get to the *Star and Journal*'s offices fast enough. 'I may be gone some time,' she told him from the door. 'I have to find my way to the station, or get a bus into London...'

'Take my car, the smaller of the two. I assume you can drive?'

He didn't even know that about her, and yet she had made passionate love with him, and only last night her body had lain intimately entwined with his!

Driving in the rain, crawling in the traffic jams to which she was completely unaccustomed, Sally sat tensely at the wheel, crying inside, yet furious, too, at the way the editor of the *Star and Journal* had, in her absence, morally and emotionally pushed her around, using her without her even having had the power to prevent or even deny his lying editorial activities.

Whether there had been any substance in those statements about Max's continuing involvement with Francine, or of his being Merry's father, she didn't even want to consider. Aunt Delia's words came back to her repeatedly... 'The real reason for Max's coming here was to see whether he and Francine might get together again.'

Bewildered by the capital city's parking regulations, she eventually and quite fortuitously found an empty space within easy walking distance of the *Star and Journal*'s main office.

'Yes,' said the receptionist, 'Mr Winterton's in. Have you got an appointment?'

'No,' said Sally through her teeth, 'but if he refuses to see me, I'll go up to his office all the same.'

Derek agreed to see her at once.

'Ah, Sally *dear*,' he said, voice loud, arms wide in a falsely warm welcome. 'Come to collect, have you, for the reports you sent in from the other side of the world? Well, you've done so well, I've upped your salary. And promoted you to chief reporter.'

'You don't take me in with your sweet talk, Mr Winterton,' she retorted, white and shaking with fury.

'You're a low-down swine, and if I had my way, you'd be out of your job tomorrow!'

He leaned back, an unpleasant smile across his face. 'So sue me, Sally dear. Litigate to your heart's content. You've got nothing to go on, nothing of substance to fling at me. I haven't once used your name, your full name, as a byline, have I?'

'Maybe, but you went as far as you dared with it. Readers need only use their intelligence and add the word "love" to the surname "Dear" that you printed, after which everybody will come to the entirely false conclusion that I wrote them.'

He rocked back on the chair's rear legs. '*Everybody?* Who the hell's heard of you?'

'Are you being deliberately obtuse, Mr Winterton? Thanks to you, and the rest of your Press *friends*, half the world, I should think. Because of my link with the famous writer Maximilian Mackenzie.'

His small eyes checked her over. 'Link, you call it? I'd say your relationship with him went a lot—er—deeper than that.'

Sally coloured furiously at his correct assumption, and Derek's smile was knowing and satisfied.

'This link you talk about—it'll come in very useful when you join us hacks and take up the new job I've given you. After working as chief reporter for the *Star and Journal*, you'll be made for life.'

'I'm not a journalist, never have been. And I wouldn't want to be one now if you offered me a million!'

'The other papers,' he went on as if she hadn't spoken, 'will all be clamouring to get you on to their payroll. Which is why I've upped your salary, to keep you out of their evil clutches. And in mine.'

'I don't want your rotten job!' she hurled at him. 'All I came for is that letter I faxed to you from Auckland, telling you I was resigning from any verbal commitment

I may have entered into with you regarding Mr Mackenzie.'

Derek affected a frown. 'You want *what*? Dear Sally, there was no letter.'

Her heart seemed to explode into tiny pieces. He was denying that letter's existence! It had been her only hope. 'But I sent it, addressed to you. It was quite a long letter, telling you—what I've just said. Since then, I haven't sent in a single report about Max. All those articles— you made them up.'

'We-ell, let's say I used a little imagination.'

'Will you repeat that,' she verbally jumped on him, 'in front of witnesses?'

'Like hell I will! Anyway, can you prove you sent that letter?'

Could she? It would be impossible.

'Got the original, or a carbon or photocopy? No? Right,' he smiled, plainly relieved, 'that's Derek Winterton in the clear.'

'But I did send it!' she shrieked, her anger mixed with a terrible anxiety. Now she wouldn't be able—ever—to clear herself in Max's eyes. Which meant it was the end of everything between her and Max Mackenzie. Surely, she racked her brains, there just had to be a way...

Her uncle! He was chairman of the board. He would help her, she was certain. How, she didn't know, but for some reason she couldn't explain, she knew she just had to see him.

CHAPTER ELEVEN

'How long will it be,' Sally asked her mother anxiously, 'before Uncle Robert comes back from abroad?' She was using the phone in Max's workroom, Ellen having told her that Mr Mackenzie had gone out and that she didn't know when he would be back.

'I don't know Robert's movements, Sally,' her mother replied. 'Oh, dear, I can hear by your voice that there's something wrong. Have you—you haven't!—broken with Max? Before Jeff and I even had a chance of meeting him?'

'No, we're still engaged, but—I can't explain, not yet. It's very important, Mum, that I see Uncle Robert.'

'You could try his secretary, dear. Surely that newspaper—what's it called——?'

'The *Star and Journal*.' Sally almost spat the words. 'Yes, they might. Thanks for your help, Mum. I'll get back to you soon.'

Reception at the *Star and Journal* obliged with the phone number of the secretary to the chairman, Mr Robert Fawcett. Eagerly Sally dialled, giving her name. 'I'd like to speak to my uncle, Mr Robert Fawcett, please.'

'Sorry, Miss Dearlove,' came the crisp feminine tones, 'but he's on the move over the next couple of weeks— Singapore first, then on to other destinations. If it's any help to you, instead of leaving his various phone numbers, he's intending to call me whenever, wherever... you know?'

Sally knew. 'Thanks all the same,' she added, 'but giving him a message from me wouldn't really be sufficient.'

'Well?' Heart pounding, she swung round. How long had Max been standing there? Even in his casual clothes, Sally thought, he looked good enough to break any woman's heart, let alone her own.

'I'm sorry about using your telephone,' she said, schooling herself to respond in his cool tones. 'I'll pay for the calls I made.'

'You will? How?' His eyebrow lifted, his raking gaze informing her that sensual thoughts were in the forefront of his mind, then his expression iced over. 'So where's this evidence you've collected that proves to me without a shadow of doubt that you were speaking the truth about not being the author of those disreputable reports?'

Shoulders drooping, Sally answered, 'Derek Winterton denied ever having received my letter.'

'That fits,' he said cynically. Hands pocketed, he walked about the room, then came to a halt in front of her. 'Nevertheless, that's your case blown sky-high. Admit it, it was an excellent ruse, wasn't it, to put off that evil moment when you'd have to confess all? That my suspicions of your motives where I'm concerned had—still have—an indisputable basis? Pity it all turned sour on you. Never in my life,' he grated, 'have I been so misled by a woman, so wrong in my judgement of her character.'

Sally tugged at his ring, thrusting it out. 'Take it.' His hands stayed where they were, in his pockets. 'Take it back, or I'll——' A sob tore at her and she flung it towards the sofa, where it bounced, then was still.

Merry must at some point have crept into the room. She looked scared and unhappy—probably, Sally guessed, having heard too much of what had just taken place.

Merry held her hand. 'Are you crying?' she whispered as Sally shakily crouched to her height. A small hand patted the moist cheeks. 'Are you missing your mummy, like me?'

'Oh, darling, I'm——' Another sob took her by surprise. I'm missing so much, she thought, Max's smile when he used to look at me, the warmth of his arms, the male power of him when he made love to me... Managing a smile, she answered, 'I'm OK, Merry, truly I am.'

'Oh, look!' exclaimed Merry, spotting the ring and going to retrieve it from the sofa. 'This is yours, Sally. Did you drop it?'

'It's not mine, Merry,' Sally corrected her, her voice strained.

'But,' the little girl looked anxiously from one to the other, 'it's always been there on your finger...'

Max lifted it from Merry's palm and eyed Sally coldly. Stop worrying the child, he was saying, stop adding to her already badly shaken sense of security because of her mother's absence. 'Will you give me your hand so that I can replace this bauble in the appropriate place?'

'Bauble', he'd called it, and it had cost him a small fortune! Was that how little he valued it, how little its significance—and that of its wearer—mattered to him?

'I can't think why,' Sally returned, 'but if it's what you want...'

'It's what I want.'

'Despite the fact that your opinion of my integrity is at rock bottom? It's the end of the road for us, Max, and you know it.'

'As I've said before, when that "end of the road" you keep referring to arrives, I'll let you know. In the meantime,' he cracked, 'I'd be obliged if you would continue to act as if you couldn't live without me.'

He lifted her hand, pushing the ring into place. In the few minutes that it had been absent, she had missed it badly. If she missed this man's ring, how would she be able to bear the empty years that stretched before her without the man himself?

'Well, is it on or off?' Gerald asked when Sally rang him three days later, 'this engagement to the great Max Mackenzie?'

'It was never really on,' she told him.

'The question is,' Gerald persisted, 'are you still wearing his ring? Judging by newspaper reports, it's some ring!'

Sally smiled sadly down at it. 'It's on loan to me, a kind of theatrical prop. A celebrated author,' she added with some bitterness, 'had to give his so-called beloved a conspicuously valuable token of his love, hadn't he?'

'You sound different,' said Gerald. I am different, Sally thought, since I last saw you, I've grown up. 'You were never bitter in the past. Sally, it's none of my business, but you haven't——?'

She stayed silent.

'You have.' He sounded saddened, but not angry.

She felt that he was due an explanation. 'When Max and I . . . Gerald, it wasn't in cold blood—at least, not on my part. I——' she steeled herself to make the confession for the first time, 'I love him, Gerald.' Now he was silent. 'Much good is it doing me! His own true love is his ex-fiancée, the mother of——'

'I never had a chance, did I?' Gerald was pursuing his own thoughts.

'I tried to tell you,' Sally pointed out gently, 'even before I went away.'

'I'm the one who's going away this time,' he stated flatly. 'Following your example, and that of many others, and travelling the world. Not long now. I've given notice at the school. But while I'm away I'll be assessing the chances of a teaching job abroad. North America, southern hemisphere, it depends what turns up.'

'I'm sorry, Gerald,' Sally answered softly, 'but——'

'That's OK. It's not just you. A man's got to start living some time.'

Merry, who had crept up to Sally and taken her free hand, tugged at it. 'Are you talking to my mummy?' she asked.

'No, poppet,' Sally whispered. 'He's called Gerald. He's a friend of mine.'

'Who's the child?' asked Gerald. 'The girl the Press alleges is the result of you-know-who's get-together with his ex-fiancée?'

'I don't know, Gerald, who her father is. I've been wondering myself, but——'

'Why not ask me?' The sharp tones coming from behind Sally took her completely by surprise. Cold chased heat up and down her spine.

'I must go, Gerald,' she said hastily.

'OK, I understand. I'll be in touch.' He rang off.

'I'm sorry,' Sally said, 'it's no business of mine——'

'Sally,' Merry sensed that trouble was brewing again, 'will you walk me round Max's pool?'

The question was so reminiscent of Aunt Delia's in New Zealand, and all the happiness she had known there, that Sally nearly wept. 'Of course, pet,' she answered, glad to escape from the castigation in Max's eyes.

'I'd like to clear up a certain matter that seems to be troubling you.' Max stood squarely, and forcefully, in her path as she made her way to her own room after settling Merry down for the night.

It was later than usual, the little girl having fought off sleep, asking, in between stories, 'When's my mummy coming?' and only reluctantly accepting Sally's vague and cautious answer 'Soon'.

'I don't know what you mean,' Sally answered quite falsely, as she knew only too well. She glanced worriedly at Merry's door, and Max sensed the reason.

'Will you come in?' He led the way into his bedroom. It was, to Sally's eyes, overly masculine, with a dark ambience that did nothing to brighten the mood. It needed a woman's touch, but she deflected the thought because she knew exactly who that woman would surely be one day. *And her name was not Sarah Dearlove.*

Max closed the door and leant against it, hands in pockets, his lean and virile physique making all her feminine instincts break into a frantic dance. His eyes moved sensually over her, taking in the partly unfastened—and erotically promising—opening of her white blouse, and the way her jeans hid nothing of her shapely hips nor the slenderness of her thighs.

'What I'm referring to,' he said, 'is the matter you were discussing so freely with your boyfriend earlier—that is, the question of the identity of Merry's father.'

'As I said,' she tossed at him, 'it's none of my business. There's no need for you to explain, but thanks for the offer.' Her steady tones seemed to stir his anger, but what he didn't know was the effort it was costing her to keep them so.

'None the less, I'll tell you the truth, so that you can pass it on to that pack of wolves you call your Press colleagues——'

'For the hundredth time,' she flung at him, 'they are *not* my colleagues!'

'No?' His searing gaze reduced her insides to a jelly, his cynicism acting on her self-esteem like corrosive acid. 'As I said, I'm taking this opportunity to put the record straight on the matter of whether or not I'm Merry's father. I state categorically that Meredith Anderley is not my child. I did not father her. *Do you understand?*' This last statement being issued through gritted teeth.

'I——' Sally held her head high. 'Why should I——' She was keenly aware how provocative her words were going to be, but had he ever paused to think how his accusations of her so-called clandestine involvement with the Press might upset her? 'Why should I believe you any more than you believe me?'

'Why, you——' Two steps from the door and she was caught in a grip of iron, slammed hard against him. His mouth twisted. 'I thought I knew myself. I thought, until you came on to my particular scene, that I was a reasonably mild man, with a temper slow to kindle, but, when aroused, never beyond my control. But you, you little schemer, you bring out a hidden, primitive side of me I never knew I had. You make me want to——'

He took a bunch of her hair and dragged her head back so that she was forced to meet his eyes head-on. Although the ferocity of his anger frightened her, it also sent a thrill of intense desire flashing through her system, and she didn't flinch when his mouth ground down on hers in a cruel and merciless kiss.

His lips were a thin line when he raised his head, his eyes burning into her very soul. 'How I was misled by your name,' he rasped, 'and by your alleged caring attitude to your parents, by your falsely sweet demeanour. I cannot forgive you for letting me down, for double-crossing me, for your undercover surveillance of my most intimate activities. Admit it, admit that your surface innocence was merely a cover for the ill intent towards me that seethed underneath.'

'It's not true,' she got out. 'You're wrong——'

But Max was in no mood to listen. 'You,' he rasped, 'have come between me and my work. I can't think straight, let alone think creatively.' He shook her. 'I have *got* to get you out of my system, and how better, *Miss Dearlove*, than the old-established way of erotic interplay between a man and a woman?'

He released her hair, appearing totally unmoved by the tears that had sprung at the pain he had inflicted, and almost tore her clothes from her, then discarding his own.

Once more his mouth ground down, bruising her lips all over again, but this time she didn't even notice the pain. Her hands clung, her arms wound their way around him, her palms rubbing over his muscle-tough torso, her nails making involuntary scratches as Max rediscovered the places that gave her the most pleasure.

When he swung her high and dropped her to his bed, she heard her throat gasping his name. The feel of his body against hers released in her a mounting sense of excitement, a fountaining of delight and throbbing need, all combining with a soaring happiness that he was there beside her, intimately with her again, and at long, long last, within her, possessing her more completely than ever he had before.

Cries escaped from her gasping throat as her body submitted to his slightest whim and every thrusting demand, his electrifying touch drawing from her more and even greater response. When she thought she would go crazy if he postponed their mutual fulfilment any longer, he relented at last and took her with him to the very limits, and beyond, of ecstasy and utter satiation.

A long time later, he let her rest, curving her into him and wrapping her pliant body in his compelling hold. She drifted into sleep, surfacing momentarily to listen to his regular breathing. So Max too was sleeping, but, drowsy though she was, she couldn't yet return to unconsciousness. Her mind drifted back to what had happened between them.

He had been rough with her, masterful and dominating, but she had not minded. He had been merciless in satisfying his masculine needs, but she had gone along with him every step of the way.

His lovemaking had left her satisfied beyond belief, lifted her to the very heights, leaving her limp with a sweet exhaustion. Yet ... *yet he had been caring enough, as before, to take precautions.* Caring, she had to concede with a touch of sadness, not necessarily out of consideration for her, but to make sure that that public image of his, which seemed to mean so much to him, remained untarnished. And to make certain, too, that she, as his *temporary* fiancée, had no reason or basis in the future, when they had gone their separate ways, to make any claims on him.

At last she drifted back to sleep, awakening in the night and reaching out, finding no one there. But she was sure he would be back. It was, after all, his bedroom. So she turned on to her side and slept again.

It was late when she awoke, disappointed to find that she was still alone. But what had she expected? He didn't love her, she had to face that. Before they'd begun, hadn't he said, almost angrily, I've got to get you out of my system? Which, Sally told herself fiercely, was what it had all been about, hadn't it?

Returning to her room, she showered and dressed. To her relief, when she went down for breakfast, she found that the kitchen was empty. In the vegetable garden, Ellen and Merry chattered to each other as they decided which of the home-grown produce to pull up and prepare for lunch.

Wondering where Max was, and what his mood might be, Sally tried to quell her excitement at seeing him again. After all, from head to toe she felt that she was more his now than ever before. Her heart beating fast, she put her head round the door of his workroom. She had hoped for a joyful reunion, for an opening of arms and a passionate return of her kisses.

Her disappointment was intense. He was not there, but it was plain that he had been. Handwritten sheets were scattered over his desk. Reference books were opened wide on every flat surface. Had he, when he had left her in the night, come down and worked through the dark hours? Had his writer's block been dispersed by their lovemaking? Had he succeeded in his stated aim last night and, by that means, eradicated her from his mind so thoroughly—exorcised her, in fact—that she had ceased to come between himself and his work?

'He rushed off first thing, Miss Sally,' Ellen told her. 'He said he was going away for a couple of days—said something about doing some background research in the north of England. He asked me to tell you.'

The phone rang in the entrance hall and she hastened to take the call. 'It's for you, Miss Sally,' she said. 'I think it's your mother.'

'I thought you'd like to know, dear,' Edie Welling said. 'Your Uncle Robert—he's home. I told him you wanted to talk to him and he said tell her she's welcome to come and see me any time. His office at the *Star and Journal*, he suggested, was probably most convenient for you. Just mention that you're his niece, and he said they'd let you go up straight away.'

'Thanks, Mum, thanks a lot.' They exchanged some family gossip and rang off.

Shining-eyed, Sally hugged Merry, who had come to stand beside her. Uncle Robert, she was sure, would help her find a way out of her difficulties.

'Was that my mummy you were talking to?' Merry asked wistfully, as if guessing the negative that was coming her way.

'No, it was *my* mummy,' Sally answered, kissing the little girl's cheek. Swinging her to the ground, she turned to the housekeeper, who was hovering.

'I'm off to London this morning, Ellen, to see my uncle. Do you think you could——' She gestured towards Merry.

'Of course, Miss Sally. I'll take good care of her. Put her to bed, if you're not home in time.'

Sally hugged Merry again. She did not know how, but deep down she hoped a miracle would happen—and miracles sometimes did—and that she would be able to prove to Max that she had after all been telling the truth about herself.

Her uncle was a widower, grey-haired and deep-voiced, a big man with an expansive manner to match. Sally had been fond of her mother's brother ever since she could remember. He had often helped his sister financially during her husband's illness, those lean years, and Sally had never forgotten his kindness.

He listened patiently and with a deep interest as Sally's story came pouring out, and it was some time later that he sat back in his chair, asking for a few minutes' silence to think matters over. Then, picking up the phone, he summoned Derek Winterton to his office.

'We'll get this sorted out somehow, Sally dear. If you'd just like to wait in my secretary's office? I won't tell the editor any more than he needs to know. Agreed?'

Gratefully, Sally nodded, keeping to herself the thought that what Derek Winterton didn't know, he simply made up.

Twenty minutes later, Robert Fawcett invited his niece back into his room.

'You be back quickly, Winterton,' he directed sharply, 'or I'll want to know the reason why.'

Derek Winterton cast a look over his shoulder that would once have made Sally curl up in fear at his possible intention. But that afternoon, with her uncle on her side, she felt fireproof from anything that Derek might do.

'Have you—um—sacked him, Uncle?' she asked tentatively.

'Not yet, Sally. Not if he comes up with the goods. He blustered a lot and said, well, yes, perhaps he did remember the letter——'

Sally gasped. 'But he absolutely denied it existed when I asked him!'

'Yes, well... At first, he told me he'd spiked it. Which, it seems, he had. Then when I threatened him with dismissal, he admitted he'd rescued it from the waste basket and filed it away. Thought that as it had come from the chairman's niece, he'd better keep it, but to you maintained the pretence that it had never arrived. Wanted to keep you on the payroll, he said. Not just because you were related to me, but because you had potential as a journalist.'

'I haven't, Uncle, really I haven't, and he knows that. And I never was on his payroll. I was trained as a teacher and I always will be a teacher. I've lost my girlish dreams of being an award-winning reporter——'

Her uncle was still laughing when the editor returned. In his hand was a sheet of paper—with the telltale hole in the centre—that set Sally's heart racing to beat the clock. It was there in his hand, the proof that would put her right with Max, restore her to his high regard, and restore also his belief in his own judgement of her character.

Before she left, she threw her arms round her beaming uncle.

Merry ran to greet her as she let herself into the entrance hall. Sally swung her high, then kissed her soundly on both cheeks.

'I'd be glad if you would put my daughter down,' a woman's voice said from the living-room door. 'There's no need for you to continue your fond nanny act now I'm here.'

'My mummy,' Merry exclaimed joyfully, 'my mummy's here!' As Sally let her down she ran to that lady's side and hung on to her hand.

Francine's eyes rested coldly on Sally's pale face. 'I've known all along, Miss Dearlove, that your so-called engagement was for publicity purposes only. Max used it as a cover to enable us to sort things out between us. The decision has been made, and I'm here. I can see no valid reason for your continuing to live in his house.'

Shivering inside, with shock and intense disappointment—her proof of her honesty and past truthfulness had plainly come too late—Sally enquired as levelly as her trembling insides would allow her, 'Are you telling me to go?' Francine stared back, head imperiously high, ignoring Merry's requests to be lifted up. 'With respect, Miss Anderley,' Sally enquired with a coolness to match her adversary's, 'are you sure you have the authority to dismiss me from Max's house?'

Francine's beautiful face lost some of its beauty. 'Max will never marry you, Miss Dearlove. First, you're not his type. Second, whatever you might—have shared with him, I can assure you was for his own private—er—masculine purposes only. Do you get my meaning?'

Sally had no alternative but to acknowledge silently that she did indeed get the lady's meaning, if only because, passionate although he had been in his lovemaking, Max had never once said he loved her. But by having the truth put into words so brutally frankly, she told herself she knew what it felt like to be on the wrong end of a machine-gun.

Francine seemed determined to press her point home. 'The reason you returned with him from New Zealand, he said, was to look after Merry. Owing to my mother's unfortunate incapacity, you stayed on here until I was able to join him. Is that correct?'

Sally nodded, sick to her depths because again it was the truth.

'Well, I'm here now. Your job is over. So...?' It was the words that were left unsaid that told Sally what she had to do.

Merry ran over to Sally's side, taking her hand and holding it tightly, as if once again she had sensed the undercurrents and guessed the direction of Sally's thoughts. 'Will you walk me round Max's pool, Sally?'

Suppressing the threatening tears at the dear and familiar words, Sally did Merry's bidding for the last time. Then she hugged the little girl and said a silent goodbye.

Sally stared out of the window of Gerald's one-bedroomed flat. He had gladly agreed to her request to take over the tenancy—landlord willing, which he had been—since Gerald had arranged to live with his parents while preparing to leave for his round-the-world trip.

It was more than a month since she had left Max's house. She hadn't heard a word from him, nor had she expected to. Only her mother knew her address, Sally having sworn her to secrecy. Sally didn't want anyone to find her, not the Press, and especially not Max Mackenzie.

From time to time she saw references to him in the papers. One report claimed that, on hearing of Francine's arrival at his home, he had rushed back from his working holiday to be with her. Another paper claimed that rumour had it that they were to become engaged again, and intended to marry in the late summer.

Seeking solace in pushing herself until she dropped, Sally had found work in the area as a supply teacher. Nights, she discovered, were the worst, when her dreams of Max consistently turned into nightmares, at which point she had woken up and desperately reached for him, only to find nothing there. If only she could see him again—just once would do. If only she could show him that letter, put herself right in his eyes, retrieving at least his good opinion, if nothing else.

It was Saturday morning. As she wandered aimlessly through the shopping centre, she stopped, as she often did, to stare at the books on show in a bookseller's windows. Sometimes Max's novels were displayed there, and her eyes would linger longingly on the studio portrait placed in a central position.

That morning his picture was there again, surrounded by his latest book, called *Diversion to Danger*. Her attention strayed to a large notice displayed to one side. 'On Saturday, April 15th, at 10.30 a.m. for one hour, Maximilian Mackenzie will be present in this shop to sign copies of his latest book.'

Stunned, Sally stared at her watch for confirmation of time and date. It was today and he was in there? In two seconds she had made up her mind. This was her last chance ever of clearing herself in his eyes.

Following some customers into the shop, she saw that the desk at which he sat was surrounded by an eager group of people, which meant that his view of the entrance door was obscured. Buying a copy of his book, she found a clear space and scribbled on a torn-out page of her personal notebook, 'I have evidence in my possession that I was telling you the truth. Now will you believe me? Sarah Dearlove.'

Heart hammering, she waited in line, thinking of the exit door and wondering if she should accept its invitation immediately. She noticed that Max gave a quick glance at each customer as he signed and returned to them their copies of his book. Not long enough, Sally thought, to take in anyone's features. Well, that was OK with her. She didn't want him to recognise her, only read her note.

Her hand was shaking as she placed the book on the table. He pulled it towards him, hand poised to write. He pushed to one side the note she had slipped inside the front cover and scrawled his signature, adding, 'With best wishes.'

As he was about to close the book, his eye must have caught sight of his name printed on the folded paper. Opening it, he read its contents. He stilled, seeming to hold his breath, then his eyes flicked up. He saw Sally's face and threw down his pen.

By the time he was round the desk and pushing through the crush, Sally was out of the shop and on the pavement, waving down a taxi. She was giving her address when a hand clamped on to her shoulder and she was bundled into the taxi's interior.

'No!' she cried, but Max was already beside her, telling the driver to proceed to the address the lady had given. 'You can't do this,' she insisted, to which his abrupt reply was,

'I can and I have.'

His distant manner precluded any further argument, and the journey passed in silence, seething on Sally's part and stony on Max's.

When they arrived outside the Victorian house where Gerald's apartment occupied the upper floor, Sally scrambled out, withdrawing money from her purse. 'Please take this man back to where you picked him up,' she said, her voice high and angry. 'He's forcing himself on me! He's got no right to——'

'As your fiancé, I have every right,' came through gritted teeth, and she was swung unceremoniously aside, the cab driver, satisfied with Max's reply, accepting smiling payment. 'Lovers' tiff, eh?' he commented, driving away with a wave.

All the way upstairs Max followed her, showing no intention of departing even as she used her key. 'I don't know why you're here,' she began, attempting to bar his way, 'but——'

'Oh yes, you do,' was his unequivocal reply.

By now he was inside, looking round, being clearly unimpressed by what he saw. He had remained forbiddingly silent through the taxi journey and he seemed no more talkative now. As Sally pulled off her jacket, he wandered round, stopping now and then to inspect and make judgements.

He surveyed her coldly. 'So since leaving my house, you've been living with your boyfriend.'

Sally frowned, knowing that Gerald had left some of his ornaments, but how could Max make that assumption from looking at them? Then she remembered the signed photograph of himself that Gerald had left on a shelf. Like the miniature of his that she hadn't had the heart to remove from her locket, she had allowed the framed photo to remain where it was.

'That picture has no significance whatsoever in my life,' she declared.

'But you couldn't wait to remove my ring.' She felt for her empty engagement finger, a gesture she had repeated a dozen times a day since returning the ring to its box and leaving it in a drawer in her room at Max's house.

She affected a careless shrug. 'It ceased to be relevant.'

'It did? I don't recall us discussing the matter.'

'Francine arrived, which left me free to go. She told me that she'd take over the care of her daughter, so there was no reason for me to stay.' She wished her heart would slacken its pace, that his nearness after so long an absence wouldn't affect her so strongly.

'Why aren't you honest and admit that you couldn't wait to get together with your boyfriend?' He looked

around. 'Is this where you're going to live when you
marry him? Or are you intending to dispense with the
marriage ceremony? After all, you're living with him
already.'

'I'm not living with him,' she protested, wanting to
beat his chest with her fists and fling her arms around
his neck at the same time. 'I never have and never will.
He's not here.'

'That much is obvious. So,' a careless shrug, 'he'll be
home soon. Is that why you're so on edge, why you
didn't want me here?'

'He's not coming, don't you understand? He's going
on a world tour. Which is what I was going to do when
I—when I first met you.' Max continued to stare at her,
his face unreadable. 'Until he goes, he's staying with his
parents. He was glad to be able to pass the tenancy over
to me. We've never been anything more than friends.
Y—you of all people should know that.' Her voice had
dropped to a whisper. 'Now will you go?' Her throat
was dry, her insides curled up with tension and longing
and sadness. This would probably be the last time she
would see him.

He strolled to the window, staring out, clearly not admiring the view.

'Go back to Francine,' Sally blurted out, 'the woman
you're really going to marry. You couldn't abandon your
background research fast enough, could you, when you
heard she was over here? You rushed to her side—that's
what the papers said. You were going to get re-engaged;
you're going to marry her later on this year.'

After a pause, in which he seemed to be absorbing
the meaning in her words, Max turned to face her. 'You,
Sally Dearlove, are actually telling me, after all you've
been through at the hands of the Press, that you believe
what you read in the papers? Let me put you right on
my movements. One,' he counted on his fingers, 'I'd

only intended going away for a couple of days. Two, my work was coming on fast. I left you that night only because the book was writing itself in my mind and I had to get it down in black and white.'

Sally nodded and moistened her lips. 'I—I saw the state of your workroom.'

'Right. Three, I went off at very short notice after an urgent phone call. Someone I wanted to see was unexpectedly available. All of which was why I had no chance to tell you.' His tone softened a fraction. 'I didn't want to wake you after——' His eyes reminisced, his very male gaze flicked over her, bringing a warmth to her cheeks. 'Four, I rushed back, yes. But not to *Francine's* side.'

She heard his words, heard the emphasis, but even then she didn't dare to hope.

'It wasn't just the papers,' she explained. 'It was what Aunt Delia told me—that the main reason for your return to New Zealand was to decide whether you and Francine might get together again.'

'Aunt Delia's a hopeless romantic. In the end, she saw how it was between us,' his hand indicated himself and Sally, 'and eliminated Francine from the plot of her particular story.'

Bewildered, still closing her ears to what her emotions were trying to get through to her, Sally persisted, 'But Francine told me the decision had been made.'

'What decision?'

'That—that you and she were going to marry. That's what I assumed.'

'Never assume. Always verify. In this case, especially,' Max strolled towards her, 'with the other person involved in the so-called "decision".' He walked away, staring at the firescreen that hid the old-fashioned grate. 'She probably wanted you to assume—as you did—that that decision was a mutual one to renew our relationship and eventually marry. Jealousy manifests itself in some strange forms.'

'But she knew about the falseness of our engagement, which meant she had no reason to be jealous of me.'

He shrugged a shoulder and touched some ornaments on the mantelpiece, moving them into better alignment with each other. 'Some years ago,' he went on, 'as you've no doubt heard, Francine and I were engaged. We were on the brink of marriage when she announced that she was pregnant. By another man.' He was silent for some time.

'That must have been a terrible shock for you,' Sally put in encouragingly.

He came out of his apparent trance and continued, 'But she still wanted me to marry her, because he refused to do so. He then disappeared out of her life.'

'You—you didn't? Marry her, I mean.'

'I did not.' Another pause. 'We remained friends, but no more. After Merry was born, Francine said she still loved the man who had fathered her child and made up her mind to search the world for him. Recently, she found him—living in Auckland. He was quite taken with Merry, discovered he loved his daughter's mother after all, and, since he was free, asked Francine to marry him. Then it was Francine's turn to be unsure.'

Max turned from his unseeing contemplation of a pencil drawing on the wall. 'In New Zealand, Francine asked my advice. I suggested she get together with him, so that they might get to know each other all over again, unencumbered by any offspring, lovable though that offspring was.'

Sally nodded in complete agreement. 'Which is why you brought Merry over here.'

'Francine was very grateful when I offered.'

'Where's Francine now?' Sally dared to ask, hearing Max's answer with a sweeping sense of relief.

'In New Zealand. Before leaving, she stayed a couple of weeks with her mother, then took Merry back with her. She and Merry's father are married at last. It seems he loves his wife and greatly regretted his former refusal to marry her.' Max's smile was genuine this time. 'As an ex-teacher of English——'

Sally shook her head. 'No "ex" about it. I've returned to teaching.'

He nodded his approval. '——and an excellent inventor of children's stories, as I know by experience, you will no doubt appreciate the twists and turns of the Francine Anderley story, not to mention its happy ending.'

'You're saying——?' Her breaths came quickly and shallowly as she looked up at him. 'You're saying that you're free of any obligation to Francine?'

'Such obligations, if they existed, ceased years ago. And I'm saying...*this*.' A stride towards her and she was gasping at the speed with which she was swung into his arms.

His mouth went down on hers, stifling her cries, and he pulled her to him as the kiss deepened and repeated itself over and over again. At first, shocked by the suddenness of his action, she stiffened her lips against the presumption of his, giving nothing.

Then, of its own accord, her mouth softened and sweetened and yielded to his, returning his kisses and parting them for his easier access. Even her arms joined in, creeping round his neck and hanging on for dear life as he swung her this way and that.

When at last he lifted his head, Sally felt as malleable as modelling clay in his hands.

'That's better,' he clipped, a warmth invading his eyes that turned her limbs to water and sent the blood racing round her body. 'Never resist me again, Miss Dearlove,' he commanded. 'Remember that in the future, I shall always demand total compliance in the woman I love, except when she's fighting me, and then...well,' his eyes glinted, 'who knows what that might lead to?'

'The woman you love?' she asked, hoarse and unbelieving. 'Who—*me*?'

He cast his eyes skywards. '*Who,* she asks! Isn't it obvious? Hasn't it been obvious almost since the moment we met?'

'N-no, it hasn't, Max. I thought—well, I believed you when you told me you wanted the engagement for your own professional reasons.'

'Oh, I did, but far more important were my own *personal* reasons. Somehow I had to keep you with me. Helping you in your difficulties wasn't enough. So I had to do it in a more subtle way.'

'Asking me to act as your assistant, in addition to acting the part of your fiancée?'

'Two ways of preventing you from making your escape. I'd found her, as the song goes, and by heaven, I wasn't going to let her go. For "her" read "you".'

'But,' she tried to ease away from him, but he wouldn't let her, 'the things you accused me of! You didn't trust me, didn't believe me. Did you?'

'I didn't,' he answered unequivocally, 'which is why I did my utmost—you'll never know how difficult that was—to keep my feelings for you in check. And strictly to myself. I felt instinctively from our first meeting that you were hiding something and that you weren't completely on the level, and my instincts proved right. I may have loved, but I also had to trust. Which is why you, my darling, gave me many bad moments.'

He kissed her lightly. 'You have to admit,' he went on, 'which you did, I remember—that at the start, your only reason for sticking to my side was to spy on me——' her attempt to jerk away was easily subdued '—and send in surreptitious reports about me to the newspaper that was employing you. And you did, did you not?' Eyebrows quirked, even now sending icicles of fear up and down her spine.

'I did, but not for long. And I've got that letter, a faxed copy of it, to prove it. Before I get it, I have another confession to make.' He let her go, and a swirl of cold air swept round her. 'I——' she cleared her throat '—I've loved you, Mr Mackenzie, right from the start. You accused me of being a fan, which I denied. Well, I have to tell you that I became a fan of yours, and not just of your books, from the moment I spied you——' she corrected herself hastily and blushingly '—saw you across the airport restaurant.'

'OK,' he put on a stubborn tone, 'where's this proof you alleged you had in that note you pushed under my nose today?'

'There's no "alleged" about it. It's here,' she searched in her bag in which she had carried the note around ever since receiving it, hoping against hope that she would one day be able to show it to him, 'in black and white. You can't argue with that.'

He took it, touching with a wry smile the hole through its centre caused by Derek Winterton's spike. As he read it, Sally tried to read his face, but he gave nothing away. Until he put it aside and looked at her.

'My darling girl,' he whispered hoarsely.

His arms opened wide and she fell into them, loving their strength and their familiarity, her heart singing at being back once again where she had longed to be ever since she had left them.

'I want you,' he groaned, running his hands over her as if she were a roughly hewn piece of sculpture and a piece of Dresden china rolled into one. 'Now.'

'At—at *this* time of day?' she croaked.

'Now,' he insisted implacably. 'To hell with the time of day. Over a month without you, of living like a monk, of dreaming each night that you were beside me, then waking to find that you weren't. The agony you've put me through. It was enough to drive a sane man mad!' He held her away. 'What shall I do with you? What,' he murmured huskily, 'would I do without you?'

'Max, that's just how I've felt without *you*. I've been so miserable, I didn't know how to bear it. And the thought that soon you'd be married to another woman— or so Francine led me to believe—it was terrible.'

'How do you think I felt, wondering where you were? I didn't even have your mother's address, let alone remember her married name, so that way of finding you was barred. I gritted my teeth and asked the editor of the *Star and Journal*, but he alleged that he had no knowledge of your whereabouts, and I think he was speaking the truth——'

'Just for once, he was,' said Sally. 'I certainly didn't tell him where I was going. But I did tell my mother.'

Max made a face. 'Much good did that do me. So I came to the conclusion, reluctantly and bitterly, that you'd run back to your boyfriend. Then, today, discovering you were living in his flat——'

'I've explained how I came to be here.'

'OK, OK. For God's sake, my darling...' He looked around, saw a partly opened door, glimpsed a bed and swung her into his arms.

In no time they were bound together with a driving desire, rediscovering each other's bodies and rejoicing in the renewal of their love. Sally knew by now how he liked her to respond, and he knew what brought her to the edge of frantic desire, and he used his knowledge to the full. They melted into each other, rested, then loved again.

'By the way,' he drawled, lifting her chin until their eyes locked, and Sally knew a moment's anxiety, 'who's this "uncle" you asked Derek Winterton in that letter to give your love to?'

'Oh,' she gave a little deprecating laugh—how would he take this, her final confession where that paper was concerned?—'that's my Uncle Robert.'

'So?' There it was again, that edgy tone that always had her worried, even now, when she knew without any doubt at all that he loved her.

'He's...you're not going to like this, darling.' She searched his eyes, but they kept the secret of his mood. 'He's the chairman of the *Star and Journal* board of directors.'

For a fraction of a second, a flicker darkened his gaze, then it was gone. His lower jaw was thrust forward in a pretence of anger. 'He is, is he? Why haven't you told me this before? Another dark secret, Miss Dearlove, that you've been hugging to that beautiful self of yours?'

'My last, Max, honestly. If it hadn't been for him, Derek Winterton wouldn't even have granted me that abortive first interview when I pleaded with him to let me join the staff of his paper. As it happened, he said, "Uncle or no uncle chairman of the board, I'm not taking on to the payroll of this paper an unworldly ex-teacher of English." Or words to that effect.'

'So the guy has *some* principles, then. He didn't bow to the chairman's attempt at nepotism.'

'Maybe not, but it was only through my Uncle Robert, my mother's brother—I'm very fond of him—that Derek Winterton produced his copy of the letter I've just shown you. You see, he'd told me that he'd thrown it in the bin.'

Max laughed. 'He very nearly did, judging by the hole in its centre.'

She looked at him askance, with just a tinge of doubt. 'You're not angry with me for having an uncle in the newspaper business?'

'If I were, my love,' was his smiling answer, 'you'd know it.'

'That much I have learnt,' she answered ruefully. 'Your temper is *ferocious*!'

He scooped her back into his arms, and it was some time later that he said, 'When we marry——' His need to kiss her overcame him and he satisfied that need yet again and at great length.

'We're getting married?' she whispered hoarsely.

'From now on, Miss *Dearlove*,' she shivered with pleasure as he once again turned her surname into an endearment, 'I'm not letting you out of my sight. By the way,' he reached across to his jacket and pulled a box from its pocket, extracting the ring, 'this goes right back where it belongs. And in a few days—*a few days, please note*—it will be joined by a plain gold band. No doubt the marketing men will make sure that our wedding will get into the newspapers. Any objections, my beautiful spy?'

A quirking brow, a satirical smile brought her fist up to make hard contact with his chest, but it changed its mind before impact and buried itself in the dark mat that spread itself across that muscular expanse.

Much later, dressed to go out for a celebratory meal, yet reluctant to leave the cosiness of the shared armchair, Max said, 'If you hadn't come to me this morning, I'd have employed a private detective agency to find you.'

'Trust a crime writer to have thought of that!'

Sally felt his laughter vibrating through her. He was right, she thought, she *had* gone to him. Something, some feeling within herself had drawn her back to that shop that morning, an invisible thread that had stretched between them ever since the moment she had tripped and fallen, projecting herself into his private space, his arms and, eventually, the rest of his life.

'Will you promise me something, Mr Mackenzie?' she asked, arms securely round his broad shoulders. 'Will you get back that book I paid for and sign it for me?'

'I will, but I'll do better than that. I'll dedicate my next book "to Sally, my wife, my *dear love* and,"' he teased, pulling her even closer, '"my real-life, beautiful undercover agent".'

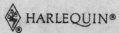

The most romantic day of the year is here! Escape into the exquisite world of love with MY VALENTINE 1993. What better way to celebrate Valentine's Day than with this very romantic, sensuous collection of four original short stories, written by some of Harlequin's most popular authors.

ANNE STUART
JUDITH ARNOLD
ANNE McALLISTER
LINDA RANDALL WISDOM

THIS VALENTINE'S DAY, DISCOVER ROMANCE WITH MY VALENTINE 1993

Available in February wherever Harlequin Books are sold.   VAL93

ROMANCE IS A YEARLONG EVENT!

Celebrate the most romantic day of the
year with MY VALENTINE! (February)

CRYSTAL CREEK
When you come for a visit Texas-style,
you won't want to leave! (March)

Celebrate the joy, excitement and
adjustment that comes with being
JUST MARRIED! (April)

Go back in time ... over the West
as it was meant to be... UNTAMED—
Maverick Hearts! (July)

LINGERING SHADOWS
New York Times bestselling author
Penny Jordan brings you her latest
blockbuster. Don't miss it! (August)

BACK BY POPULAR DEMAND!!!
Calloway Corners, involving stories of
four sisters coping with family, business
and romance! (September)

FRIENDS, FAMILIES, LOVERS
Join us for these heartwarming love stories
that evoke memories of family and
friends. (October)

Capture the magic and romance of
Christmas past with HARLEQUIN
HISTORICAL CHRISTMAS STORIES!
(November)

WATCH FOR FURTHER DETAILS IN ALL HARLEQUIN BOOKS!

CALEND